# RAID

## AND THE BLACKEST SHEEP

## HARRI NYKANEN

Translated by
Peter Ylitalo Leppa

Ice Cold Crime LLC

Disclaimer: This is a work of fiction. All characters, names, incidents and situations depicted in this work are wholly the creation of the author's imagination or are used fictitiously. Any resemblance to actual events, organizations, places or persons, living or dead, is entirely coincidental and beyond the intent of the author, the translator, or the publisher.

Originally published in Finnish as Raid ja Mustempi Lammas by WSOY, Helsinki, Finland. 2000.

Translated by Peter Ylitalo Leppa

Published by
Ice Cold Crime LLC
5780 Providence Curve
Independence, MN 55359

Printed in the United States of America

Cover by Ella Tontti

Ice Cold Crime LLC gratefully acknowledges the financial assistance of:

FINNISH LITERATURE EXCHANGE

Library of Congress Control Number: 2010937155

ISBN-13: 978-0-9824449-2-4
ISBN-10: 0-9824449-2-3

## Also by Harri Nykanen:

In Finnish:

*Kuusi katkeraa miljoonaa.* WSOY, 1986.
*Juudaspeli.* WSOY, 1987.
*Joku pelkää kirjettäsi.* WSOY, 1988.
*Takapiru.* WSOY, 1989.
*Paha paimen.* WSOY, 1990.
*Huumekyttä: rikospoliisin muistelmat.* WSOY, 1991.
*Raid.* WSOY, 1992.
*Raid ja paperiansa.* WSOY, 1994.
*Raid ja lihava mies.* WSOY, 1997.
*Raid, kolmoisnide.* WSOY, 2000.
*Raid ja mustempi lammas.* WSOY, 2000.
*Raid ja pelkääjät.* WSOY, 2001.
*Raid ja legioonalainen.* WSOY, 2002.
*Raid ja poika.* WSOY, 2003.
*Puoli volttia kerien ja muita rikosnovelleja.* WSOY, 2003.
*Kilikalikeikka- ja muita juttuja rikosten poluilta.* Johnny
    Kniga, 2003.
*Ariel.* WSOY, 2004.
*Ariel ja hämähäkkinainen.* WSOY, 2005.
*Johnny & Bantzo.* WSOY, 2005.
*Raid ja tappajat.* WSOY, 2006.
*Valhe.* WSOY, 2007.
*Johnny & Bantzo osa 2: Operaatio Banana split.* WSOY,
    2008.
*Johnny & Bantzo osa 3: Viimeinen hippi.* WSOY, 2009.
*Jumalan selän takana.* WSOY, 2009.


Harri Nykanen's books have been published in several
other languages.

# RAID

## AND THE BLACKEST SHEEP

# Cast of Characters

Raid.................................................Hit man

Nygren.................................…..Aging criminal

Jansson............Helsinki PD detective lieutenant

Huusko............................Jansson's colleague

Susisaari...........................Jansson's colleague

Koistinen........................................Preacher

Kempas….....Head of Helsinki PD undercover unit

Leino...............................Kempas' colleague

Lunden.............................Kempas' colleague

Anna..................................Physical therapist

Rusanen...........................…......Northern drug lord

Hiltunen...........Ex-con, served time with Nygren

Sariola….."Shorty," Nygren's former accomplice

Lehto...……"Slim," Nygren's former accomplice

# 1.

Raid drove while Nygren slept in the back seat.

Nygren had folded up his wool overcoat beneath his head and curled up his thin legs. His hands were tucked against his chest. One knee was thrust against the back of the driver's seat and Raid could feel it pressing against the small of his back. Nygren's dark-blue, nearly black sport coat was unbuttoned, and a burgundy tie with white polka dots spilled over the edge of the seat.

Nygren was approaching sixty. His face was lean and furrowed with an inch-long scar at the left corner of his mouth. With his blond hair combed straight back to the nape of his neck, Nygren almost looked boyish. The expensive watch on his wrist topped off his stylish attire.

Nygren wore a tranquil expression, like that of a man who does only what he believes in.

Raid enjoyed driving, especially Nygren's car—a classic V8 Mercedes. It had been meticulously cared for, and probably kept under a sheet in a heated garage for the last two decades. Despite being thirty years old, it looked almost pristine. The odometer read just under 60,000 miles and the black leather upholstery showed little sign of wear. The chrome knobs on the radio begged to be turned.

Half way between Helsinki and Turku, it began to rain. Nygren opened his eyes. They were alert—not at all bleary. Still, Raid was sure that only a moment before, Nygren had been fast asleep.

"The sound of rain…something about it."

Nygren cranked down the rear window a bit and took a deep breath. A cold wind swept inside, tossed his hair and sprinkled his face with rain.

"Something about it… Where are we?"

"Just past the half-way mark."

"Let's take the scenic route the rest of the way."

Nygren sat up enough to dig a pack of cigarettes from the inside pocket of his coat.

"I'm paying you well enough that I'm sure you won't mind."

He lit his cigarette with a vintage Zippo lighter. Raid could smell the fumes from the lighter fluid.

Nygren held up the lighter.

"My entire inheritance from my father… It was in his breast pocket when he took some shrapnel from a Russian grenade."

He pointed to a dent in the case.

"That's where this came from—saved his life. An object has no value without a story, and there's a good one behind this lighter. It gives it a reason for being."

Nygren patted the back seat.

"This car too has a story. And this coat…and this watch."

He slid a pair of sunglasses out of the pocket of his overcoat and put them on.

"Ray-Ban. I'll tell you the story about these sometime. We'll have some good times together."

"I'm sure," said Raid.

"For now, I'm paying you to listen. But sooner or later you'll be paying me to talk."

A few drags later, the cigarette was half gone. Nygren cranked the window all the way down and flicked out the butt. He put his head out of the car and savored the wind. Raid caught a glimpse of the man's solemn face in the driver's-side mirror and fought back the urge to smile.

Nygren pulled his head back inside and fixed his tousled hair with a few quick strokes of his fingers.

"I've had my hair cut the same way for thirty years. During that time, it's been in style three different times. What does that tell you?"

"What?"

"That once you've found your style, you should stick with it. But I don't suppose you worry too much about fashion."

"Don't suppose I do," said Raid.

"And you're no chatterbox either. A word here, a word there. Hardly verbal fireworks. You know I'm a social man and I enjoy listening. I trust that you have plenty of stories to tell—true stories, no less."

"I promised to listen, not talk. Besides, you've been sleeping the whole trip."

"When you get to be my age, you need a nap every so often."

Nygren pulled himself into a sitting position. He leaned forward and studied Raid in the rear-view mirror.

"Are you sure you're with me the whole way... To the end?"

"That's what I promised."

"Promises have been broken."

"Not by me."

Nygren's expression softened. He seemed relieved.

\* \* \*

The Elia Church was situated in an old movie theater in Turku, on the west coast of Finland. With its grungy 1950s style building, it was far removed from some of the grand medieval structures in the city.

The sound of music and singing carried all the way outside. Not your typical downcast, guilt-ridden Finnish hymn, but a Finnish version of a cotton fields gospel song. Nygren stopped outside the door to listen. He nodded his head to the rhythm, and soon his arms joined in too. His clapping hands were one with the tempo. He even ventured a few little dance steps.

"Hallelujah, shall we get started?"

Raid opened the door and Nygren stepped inside.

They passed through a long hallway and came to a row of coat hooks on the right and a pair of birch-veneered doors on the left. At the end of the hallway was a rear entrance that had been used when the movie theater was still in operation. A green exit sign still hung over the door.

Nygren swung open both birch doors and stepped into the auditorium. He stood at the end of a corridor that divided the room in two. In his long black open coat, he looked like a gunman preparing for a showdown. Raid fell in behind him on the right.

"Jesus paid dearly with his own blood for your sake. Do not let worldly glory throw you off the path of righteousness, nor tempt you away from your heavenly home…"

The pastor was slightly younger than Nygren and was dressed in a stylish, light-gray suit. A thick gold bracelet and a stout gold ring rounded off his expensive getup. His hair, already graying slightly, was neatly trimmed and carefully combed. His face was tanned and smooth, but something about his outward appearance seemed contrived.

The pastor's persona was like a caricature of some Texas governor obsessed with appearing to voters as though he was able to do anything a man ought to: dance briskly, ride a horse, hit a golf ball three hundred yards and, as a bonus, savor the fruits of the best whorehouses in the state.

The pastor took a glass of water from the lectern in front of him and took a couple of swallows. Refreshed, he surveyed his lambs with a charismatic expression.

"For Jesus tells us, 'Ask and it shall be given you.' For everything you have given, you will receive many times over—twice, three times, even five times as much."

"Hallelujah! Thank you Jesus," said a woman in the front row, her head bowed and her hands clasped in front of her chest. Her words infected the others and a wave of hallelujahs moved through the crowd.

"You are the body of the kingdom of heaven and I am the soul. The soul must guide the body, and the body must feed the soul. There are millions upon millions who thirst for the word of God, and we have been chosen to spread that word to the corners of the earth. We have been entrusted with a fund-raising goal…and we will fulfill it."

The pastor looked expectantly at the congregation.

"We will fulfill it," the congregation repeated.

"Our goal is to collect one hundred and fifty thousand euros amongst ourselves so that we can print Bibles for pagan countries, countries where cows are gods or where people bow down to trees and graven images. This evening, the collection…"

A young woman was sitting behind the piano wearing a chaste baby-blue frock and an even more chaste ribbon of the same color in her blond hair. She was the first to notice the outsiders as she raised her timid, curious gaze from the keys. Soon after, another turned to look and then a third.

"…will go, in its entirety, toward our fund-raising goal. So open your hearts generously and set aside some treasure for your heavenly home…"

Nygren took a few steps forward and Raid followed.

"Hallelujah, brother Koistinen," said Nygren in an outwardly confrontational tone.

The pastor raised his eyes as the rest of the congregation turned to look at their visitors. A brief shock ran across the pastor's face before he gathered his composure.

"Hallelujah, dear brother…and who might you be? The Lord's blessings to you both, and welcome. Please join us—we always keep an open door for visitors."

"We're in a hurry, sadly. So many sick, and the healers so few. I only came to collect my debt—then my friend and I will be on our way."

The congregation turned inquiringly back to their shepherd.

"There must be some misunderstanding. If you'd be so kind as to leave—you're interrupting our services here."

The pastor motioned discreetly with his hand, and a man sitting in the back row stood up. Undoubtedly the bouncer, he walked in a slight forward hunch, like an old wrestler. Accustomed as he was to people crumbling at his feet, he couldn't imagine anything else happening.

In a single motion, Raid whirled, pulled a gun from somewhere beneath his coat, and leveled it at the man's forehead. The bouncer managed one more step before he got the message. He froze in his tracks and glanced helplessly at Pastor Koistinen.

Nygren dug a paper out of his coat pocket, unfolded it and waved it in the air.

"I have a document here that says you owe me fifteen thousand euros. Don't you remember? I lent it to you six years ago in Stockholm, when you started up that casino. Plenty of girls there too, though not as pretty as these."

Nygren smiled at the pianist and she instinctively smoothed her hair.

"How many years have I been after you, and here I find my lost black sheep in beautiful Turku, in such pleasant company. Last time I was here was ten years ago when I did two years in that nice house on the hill, where the blinds are made of iron, as the old song goes."

"I don't even know you…"

Nygren rifled through his pocket again and pulled out a photograph. "You deny me as Peter denied Christ. 'Before the cock crows, thou shalt deny me thrice.'"

"It's a lie… This… It's all lies…"

"Is it?"

Nygren tapped on the photograph with his finger.

"Here we are, sitting like best pals over good Bavarian beers. You remember when we stopped at that nice whorehouse in Hamburg? This naked girl here...name was Hanne as I remember...or something like that..."

Nygren handed the photo to a woman sitting nearby.

"Pass it around."

The woman gaped at the picture before passing it to the man sitting next to her.

"This good shepherd of yours has always been interested in the ladies. He once lived with a Brazilian stripper for six months. Uh, you know...the kind that dances around naked? Now, where might that girl be right now? Maybe she went back to the Amazon delta or died of an overdose in some Stockholm alleyway."

Koistinen's poise began to fail and he leaned against the lectern.

Nygren continued to turn the screw.

"Let's just settle our little money issue so you can go about business as usual. Business is really all this is about..."

Nygren let his gaze wander over the congregation.

"Were I a sheep, I'd be one of the blackest, but the only thing I take from anybody is money. You take their souls. These people put their faith in you, put themselves and their lives in your hands, and you betray them. That's the kind of thing you burn in hell for, you know. You're one evil shepherd, Koistinen."

Koistinen played yet another card, and did so with the professionalism only twenty years of experience as a scam-artist can bring.

"Out of our midst, you spawn of the devil. I'll not allow you to pollute my flock with your dirty lies. Jesus paid dearly for…"

Suddenly he stiffened, his breathing faltered and his eyes seemed to bulge out of their sockets. He mashed his lips together a few times, then let out a stream of words, with no emphasis or rhythm, as though read from a dictionary one after another.

"Alema, isa, nader, elia, abba, Israel…"

"And now you can even speak in tongues. Last time we met, all you knew was Finnish, and some fucking terrible Swedish."

Nygren walked up to Koistinen and slapped him hard on the cheek.

Koistinen's rapid-fire monologue came to a halt, as though cut with a scissors.

Nygren's hand dove into his pocket again.

"I have a few more pictures…"

He walked back toward the crowd and passed out the pictures left and right. Then he returned to the altar and seized Koistinen by the tie, jerked him closer and turned toward the congregation.

"After that miraculous display of speaking in tongues, Pastor Koistinen has yet another miracle for you. He'll show you how to stop a bullet with the strength of his faith."

Raid drew a second gun from beneath his coat. With the other gun still trained on the wrestler, he aimed it at Koistinen's forehead.

Nygren jostled Koistinen, now limp and impassive.

"Ready for the bullet-stopping miracle?"

Koistinen searched Raid's eyes for a hint of mercy, but found none.

"Don't. I'll pay," he whispered to Nygren. "In the back room."

Nygren looked at the congregation.

"He wants to pay, but you want a miracle. One against many—majority rules. Let's have a miracle."

Raid cocked the hammer with his thumb.

Koistinen abandoned his preacher role in favor of survival.

"Tell me what I have to do."

Nygren's voice was almost affectionate.

"Can't you perform one little miracle? Doesn't your faith move mountains and raise the dead?"

"No."

"But don't you speak in tongues and have daily talks with God like he was a friend of yours?"

"No. You know that."

"Louder!"

Nygren leaned in and cupped his hand to his ear.

"I can't."

Nygren's voice filled the theater. "Why not? How can you speak in tongues then?"

"It's an act."

"So speaking in tongues was an act. What about all this?"

Nygren swept his hand over the congregation in an arc.

"Everything is…"

"Everything is what?"

"An act."

"So you're a fraud. Do I understand you correctly?"

"Damnit Nygren, we were friends once…"

"Do I understand you correctly?"

"Yes…"

Nygren forced Koistinen to his knees and took a handful of his hair.

"You heard him. He's a fraud, sadly. The worst kind. A ravening wolf in sheep's clothing. Men like him are shepherds as long as the sheep have wool to shear and meat to grind. After that, he'll leave his flock to the beasts. He piles his burdens on others' backs, but carries none himself. He dictates what you can do, but heeds no rules himself."

Koistinen tried to jerk free, but Nygren tightened his grip.

"Ask their forgiveness. Ask your followers for forgiveness."

"Goddamnit, Nygren…"

Koistinen tried to stand, but Nygren shoved him down.

"Ask for forgiveness!"

"Please forgive me."

"You're a swindler and a false prophet. What are you?"

"A swindler…a false prophet."

"And a ravening wolf in sheep's clothing."

"And a ravening…wolf in sheep's clothing."

Nygren let go and Koistinen nearly fell on his face.

"Get up!"

Koistinen stumbled to his feet looking drugged.

Nygren scanned the hushed crowd. Not the slightest hint of self-satisfaction or triumph showed on his face. On the contrary, he looked saddened.

"Try not to be so gullible. The world is full of false prophets from the same stock as myself and this black-souled brother Koistinen. Be skeptical, but don't stop searching. Maybe you'll find a good

11

shepherd yet. Remember that a tree is known by its fruit, and a bad tree bears no good fruit."

Nygren stepped down from the lectern, looking every bit as old and stiff as he was.

Outside, it was already dusk and the rain had just picked up. Nygren flipped up the collar of his coat and stepped out of the foyer into the rain.

"What'd you think?"

"An impressive show."

"I didn't read the Bible in prison for nothing... Mom always wanted me to be a preacher."

"You'd have been a good one," said Raid.

* * *

Raid drove and Nygren sat in the back seat. Nygren watched the landscape disappear into the darkness. He hadn't said a word for more than half an hour, but that suited Raid just fine.

"You still with me, Raid?"

"Don't doubt me, Thomas."

"To the end?"

"To the end."

# 2.

"Bend to the side...down...up...now to the right. Stand up straight, Jansson... Down...up...left...right. Jansson, can't you straighten your back anymore?"

The instructor was blonde, about forty years old, and the water slid across her hips as she waded over to Jansson. She placed one hand on his back and the other on his belly. Despite her slenderness, her arms were strong. She looked at Jansson and smiled.

"Relax. Don't be so stiff."

Jansson glanced over at the row of amused faces on the pool deck. Huusko laughed aloud.

"Listen to the girl, don't be so stiff. A man oughta have only one stiff spot, and it's not your back."

"Stop it, Huusko," she snapped, but watered down her scolding with a smile.

Jansson waded to the edge of the pool and pushed himself up. The water gave his body buoyancy, making the feat seem effortless.

"I've had enough."

"Just messin' around," said Huusko.

After a quarter mile of swimming, Jansson could have sworn his body was more muscular. But one glance at his stomach told him the feeling was an illusion; the same sixty pounds of excess fat were in the same place as always. Still, his back felt better.

"How can such a big man give up so easy?" the instructor prodded.

"Hey, big man, wait for me at the bar," Huusko shouted as Jansson padded off.

"You're here to get in shape, not to get drunk," the instructor said.

"Why not both?"

Jansson sat in the sauna for a few minutes before stepping into the shower. Then he put on a robe, tucked his towel and shaving kit under his arm and set off down the long hallway toward his room, all the way at the end on the right-hand side. Huusko's was just across the hall. Once inside, Jansson's first order of business was to pour himself a shot of whiskey, then he collapsed onto the bed.

The room was intended for two, but there were enough vacancies that Jansson had gotten it to himself. It featured a wardrobe, nightstand, chair, television and a phone. A sappy landscape print hung on the wall. Clean, but impersonal. A month earlier, the room had been remodeled and it still smelled of paint. The rest of the building was still a construction zone.

The window was slightly ajar and Jansson heard a loud argument from the front yard. He picked up his tumbler and went to have a look. A maintenance man was disputing a young construction worker's choice of parking spots for his trailer.

The front yard of the physical rehabilitation center was expansive. Nearest the building was an asphalt parking lot for guests. The maintenance man didn't deem contractors as guests, and even though barely a dozen cars were parked in the front lot, he insisted on ushering the trailer to the rear.

The building was situated in the middle of a gloomy, boulder-ridden spruce forest. With his rehabilitation only on its third day, Jansson was already feeling distressed. How in the hell could he possibly endure two weeks?

In reality, Jansson's back wasn't in such bad shape. He had strained it while turning his compost pile. The department's doctor had examined him and criticized his excess weight and lack of exercise. Jansson couldn't help but admit the doctor had a point, and he had promised to do something about it. For lack of anything better to say, he had inquired about physical rehabilitation.

To Jansson's surprise, a few days later he received a written notice informing him that he was now enrolled in a physical rehab program. The center was owned by a union affiliated with the Social Democratic Party and was apparently trying to find customers, even if by force. The center's state funding was determined by its enrollment, so with some shrewdness and cunning, any government employee who didn't put up much of a fight was being funneled into the program. Half of the police force had been through the same regimen, Huusko more than any other, though his only ailments were the occasional hangover and chronic sweaty feet.

Either the police doctor was a henchman for the Social Democratic Party or a shareholder of the center. Nothing else could explain such enthusiasm for its services.

Jansson had been wary of rehab from the start. It seemed to him that the patients were treated like brainless cretins, ordered to perform strange gesticulations for no justifiable reason.

For Jansson, these water aerobics were little more than ritual humiliation.

Or perhaps he just had an attitude problem. Huusko and the others seemed to be enjoying themselves. The food was free as well as healthy, they were still getting paid, and there was always someone on hand to listen to the patient's self-diagnoses for aches, pains and joint wear.

Even so, Jansson had been stubbornly resistant from the beginning. To top off the boredom, his conscience bothered him; he felt he was defrauding the public. Jansson put the blame, at least in part, on Huusko, who had painted a tempting but distorted picture of physical rehab. Jansson still couldn't understand how Huusko had managed to lure him out to the middle of nowhere. But Huusko wasn't the only culprit—Jansson blamed his wife, too. Had she been as suspicious and contrary as usual, he never would have gone.

"Of course you should go, if it's free," she had said. "You'll get some exercise and healthy food, and you can rest and take care of yourself. You're not getting any younger. Anyway, I warned you about overexerting yourself."

Even Captain Tuomela hadn't tried to deter him, though Jansson was in the middle of a murder investigation that was all over the tabloids.

"There's no statute of limitation for murders," Tuomela had said. Jansson thought his boss had been suspiciously generous.

The first night there, Jansson figured out why Huusko had been so eager about rehab. There was a certain nurse he knew from before. Their affair had been hot, but fleeting.

The woman had cared for Huusko after he sustained a gunshot wound five years earlier. Huusko had stopped a man suspected of a recent stabbing when, without warning, the man pulled a gun and shot him three times. Though the weapon was only a .22, one of the bullets had hit him in the heart.

For a moment, Huusko had breathed his last, but a doctor had revived him in the back of an ambulance. A quick surgery had saved his life. Another bullet had hit him in the shoulder blade and the wound had required a month of physical rehab. A man like Huusko couldn't bear such a close relationship with an attractive woman without trying something.

The nurse's husband had discovered the relationship and filed for divorce. Afterwards, she had moved from Helsinki to the small town near the physical rehab center and began practicing there.

Jansson glanced at his watch. Ten past three. Only three hours since lunch and he was already hungry. The food at the clinic was light and healthy. For lunch, they had had cabbage soup, and the dinner menu included steamed rainbow trout and vegetable stew. Jansson was sure he would suffer from withdrawal if he didn't get a proper steak dinner soon, but the nurses had imposed a strict diet and monitored it aggressively.

At half-past three, Jansson called his wife at work to complain about the conditions and slow passage of time, but he didn't get the sympathy he was looking for. As she was just on her way to a meeting, she cut the conversation short. Jansson promised to call back in the evening.

Feeling vaguely restless, Jansson got dressed and

went to look for something to do.

Half a dozen war veterans were sitting at a table near the window in the lobby, clinking coffee cups and sipping lemonade.

The recreation area featured a billiards table, ping-pong and a small library and reading room. Jansson picked up a copy of *Technology Today* and tried to focus on reading, but when he realized he had been staring at the same paragraph without reading a single word, he tossed it aside.

Jansson felt abandoned. His wife didn't care to talk to him and Huusko spent his time chasing his physical therapist. He felt alone, as if in the middle of a dark forest, useless and forgotten.

Jansson was in search of a suitable scapegoat for all his recent troubles.

"You're not getting any younger."

Jansson clung to his wife's every word.

He was fifty-four. Did she think he was too old? She was only four years his junior, after all.

Jansson was slowly coming to terms with the fact that his despondency had stemmed from his wife's comment. Ordinarily, he wouldn't have given it a second thought, but at that moment, it had struck a nerve and lingered, gnawing at his mind.

He had strained his back while slaving away at the compost pile, despite his wife's warnings. Her sarcastic reminders about it hurt more than she realized. Jansson himself had noticed how heavy his breathing had been while climbing the stairs. His wife described his gait as a crawl. Even the suggestion of any slightly more complicated sexual positions had made her laugh in his face.

That laugh had sent both his prowess and passion reeling.

Jansson had convinced himself that he was just out of shape, but after her remarks, he had had to admit to himself that his age was as much to blame.

The previous week, a colleague—two years his junior—had undergone bypass surgery. Jansson and Huusko had been to see him at the hospital.

As they left the hospital, Jansson had heard Huusko whispering to himself: Good luck with retirement, Gramps.

Though the comment had grated on Jansson, he hadn't said a word, but Huusko had noticed.

"Did I say something wrong?"

"I'll let you know when you don't."

"You know I got a good heart. I only hurt people by accident."

"Huusko, you really think Leppä's a gramps?"

"He didn't hear that."

"*I* did. He's a year and a half younger than I am."

"He looks a lot older," was Huusko's slippery response.

"I don't buy it."

"You wanna know what I think?"

"No."

"I think you're one of those 'forever-young' types."

"I don't want to be young."

"And not old either?"

"Not yet."

That's when Huusko had started to coax Jansson into coming along to the rehab center. People would see Jansson as a new man, he promised.

Jansson walked into the lobby where the patients

were gathering for dinner. The trout smelled fishy, and in the worst way.

It crossed Jansson's mind that his wife and his colleagues might be conspiring against him.

Huusko entered the lobby swinging a duffle bag and wearing a gray tracksuit, running shoes and his trademark black leather jacket. His step was light, his manner unspoiled by any trace of worry. He had come from the direction of the staff dormitories— Jansson could guess which room.

Huusko spotted Jansson standing by the bulletin board, studying it with his arms crossed.

"I found something for us to do tonight."

"For us or you?"

"You think I'd forget the man on whose goodwill my entire future hangs? Got us a window table at the Millhouse Tavern. Tonight we'll have meat."

"Didn't you already get some?"

"C'mon, I'm talking about food. They got pepper steaks with creamy garlic mashed potatoes on the menu. On the way back we can stop by the deli for meat pies and fried sausages."

"Sounds good. We taking a taxi?"

"Yup. To celebrate payday."

Jansson returned to his room and chose his best outfit: black pressed pants and a dark blue nautical blazer.

Jansson had laid his clothes on the bed when his cellphone rang on the nightstand. The caller was unidentified—the display read only an asterisk.

"Jansson."

"Kempas here. I heard you're at rehab. Your old bones bothering you?"

Kempas was a veteran lieutenant in charge of the

Helsinki Police Department's undercover operations. He had a reputation for being difficult.

"Was there something you wanted to talk about?"

"I hear you know a torpedo by the name of Raid."

For some reason, Kempas' style grated on Jansson.

"So?"

"Working on a case over here and ran across his name. We need some background on him."

"What case?"

"He's travelling with Nygren, an old ex-con. I'd like to know why."

"And I'm supposed to know?"

"I've been told you know Raid better than anyone in the department. They say you're almost pals."

"Not enough that he calls me up to give regular updates."

"Can't you venture a guess?"

"Raid sells protection. Maybe he's along as a bodyguard."

"Nygren's never needed one before."

"Sorry, that's my best guess."

"Maybe Raid's helping Nygren with a job? Nygren has a record in Sweden too. Hasn't Raid been living in Sweden for quite some time?"

"There and Denmark."

"Maybe they know each other from there."

"Maybe."

"Well, we could use the names of anyone in Finland who knows Raid, and of course, anything else pertaining to him. You're the one who investigated the Imatra Castle Hotel and warehouse shootings. Wasn't Raid a suspect in those?"

"Yeah, but tell me this... If Nygren and Raid

haven't done anything wrong, why are you after them?"

"If Nygren hasn't done anything yet, he's about to. The guy's been in the business for almost forty years, and I'd just as soon the bastard spent his retirement in a cell."

"What do you have against Nygren?"

"Cops hate crooks like cats hate mice."

Jansson's heart went cold. He knew Nygren, and didn't consider him the worst of criminals. A career criminal, yes, but in his own way, he was entertaining.

The first time Jansson met Nygren had been nearly twenty years earlier, while investigating a gunfight in an illicit Helsinki gambling house that attracted a host of shady characters.

Nygren had been working the card table when a fight broke out among the gamblers. Two were shot; one of them was Nygren, who took a bullet in the stomach and nearly died.

Jansson suspected that Nygren was the second shooter. There had to have been two, since two types of bullet casings had been found. The guns, however, were never recovered. When the shooting occurred, there were about twenty people in the casino, but all had fled before the police arrived. Only the wounded were left.

As soon as Nygren's condition had stabilized, Jansson interrogated him, but to no avail. The other victim had kept his mouth shut as well. The case had remained unsolved and had often troubled Jansson over the years.

Nygren's rakish style and sense of humor had made an impression on Jansson. In a way, he was a kind of gentleman criminal with his own moral code, which he stuck to.

In Jansson's opinion, Nygren wasn't violent, though he'd been involved in a couple of big cases. He was a suspect in a Stockholm robbery three years earlier, in which eight million kronor were stolen from the central train station. Sufficient evidence against Nygren was never found.

"I don't think I'll be of much help," Jansson replied.

"Alright if I call you back when we find out more?" Kempas asked.

"Suit yourself."

"Get better."

"You too."

Dressed in his best, Jansson crossed the hall and knocked on Huusko's door. Huusko was still in his underwear with a towel around his neck. A half-empty bottle of vodka and a barely-touched bottle of grapefruit juice were on the table.

"Help yourself."

"Apparently you've already helped yourself to a few."

"Working on the third, all pretty weak."

Huusko's clothes were uniformly scattered across the floor. By his carefree organizational system, it was easy to tell he was still a bachelor.

Jansson took the clothes that were spread out on the chair, piled them on the bed and sat down.

Huusko put on a pair of tight black jeans. The scar from his heart surgery seemed to have been cut with a scythe. Despite his unhealthy eating habits, Huusko's upper body was as muscular as any athlete's. Huusko noticed Jansson sizing him up enviously, and he flexed his right bicep.

"Solid steel!"

"Right, right…"

Huusko did a few shadowboxing steps, parried and counter-punched, then calmed down and pulled on a dark-blue jean shirt. He stopped to appraise Jansson's outfit.

"Skipper look? Nice try, but the cowboy look is in right now. Check out my genuine Texas boots—and don't drool."

"Kempas called."

"Let's forget work, huh?"

"He asked about Raid."

Huusko didn't seem to be listening. He finished off his shot of vodka, then poured the rest into a plastic flask.

"C'mon, let's go."

The veterans were at the table rehashing World War II. They had just gotten through the Battle of Summa and were starting into the Battle of Ihantala, the largest battle in Nordic history. There, Finnish forces had halted a Soviet advance despite being outnumbered three to one.

Jansson said hello to a few of the vets he'd gotten to know. The taxi was already waiting outside the door.

One fellow who'd been in the spa with Jansson noticed the taxi.

"You boys off to the dances?"

"We're coming too," said another.

"You guys stick around and hold down the fort," said Huusko.

"I hear they're supposed to have a live band tonight," said Jansson's friend.

The dance floor was open every night, but only on Wednesdays and Fridays did they have live music.

"Have fun tonight," said Jansson.

"Not too much, though," added Huusko.

"Don't drink too little," shouted one of the vets.

The Millhouse Tavern was in the heart of town, half a mile away. The low building had been built in the seventies, just as the town's central area shifted to a new area. Next to it were the social security office, a bank, a liquor store, a supermarket and a hardware store.

The interior of the tavern was trying for a sort of earthy, cabin feel. German-style painted elves, about as charming as a painted toilet, had been hung all about.

Huusko ordered two beers at the bar and brought them to the table. The place was nearly empty.

"Why is Kempas interested in Raid?" asked Huusko, puffing at the froth at the top of his glass.

"Was it hard for you to wait till now?"

"Not at all."

Jansson told him.

"Kempas is a good cop, but he's no nice guy. A killjoy, you might say."

A small red car stopped in the parking lot. Huusko sat up as a blonde-haired woman stepped out of the car wearing a grey skirt and a thin blue jacket. She was about forty years old. She pulled a flat handbag out of the car, closed the door and headed toward the restaurant in swinging strides. It was the same nurse who, in the pool that morning, had faulted Jansson's posture.

"Some broads really know how to walk," said Huusko.

The woman stopped at the entrance and looked around. After noticing Huusko, she came to the table. Huusko played the gentleman, took her coat and offered her a chair.

"Plenty of space for a beautiful woman. You two know each other, right? Boss, this is Anna. Anna, this is my boss, Lieutenant Jansson."

Jansson shook her hand, but she avoided his eyes. He tried to seem friendly and carefree, not wanting her to think he'd been bothered earlier.

Huusko scuttled off to get her a drink.

"Huusko tells me you've lived here for quite a few years. You must enjoy it?" said Jansson.

"I'm from around here... Nothing wrong with the place, and if I get bored, Helsinki's just over an hour away."

She fiddled with the diamond ring on her middle finger.

"Is this your first time at a rehab center?"

"Do I look like it is?"

She laughed.

"No comment. Are you enjoying yourself?"

Jansson paused.

"If I said yes, I'd be lying. Three days in and I'm already running out of reasons to stay. At this rate I'll end up drowning myself in the hot tub."

She laughed again. A few wrinkles showed on her face, but her smile softened them.

"Some people come again and again...feel right at home."

"I suppose that depends on what home is like."

"You don't seem to have anything to complain about in that department."

"Could be worse."

Huusko returned with two fresh beers and a drink for the lady.

"We figured we'd have steaks. You're not gonna tattle, are you?"

"Depends on the bribe... I'll have to leave at eight, unfortunately. I have a new fitness program that has to be ready by tomorrow. But you guys can stay as long as you like, I'll drive myself..."

Jansson looked at the woman, then at Huusko. Maybe their spark wasn't as hot as Huusko had hoped. Though Jansson always stood up for his team, he had to admit that this woman had just the kind of sensitivity and style that would go to waste on a guy like Huusko. Apparently, it went to waste on this whole little town.

Huusko looked disappointed.

"The band doesn't start till nine. I won't get to dance with you."

"Another time."

"How 'bout now."

Huusko dug some change out of his pocket and weaved his way over to the jukebox. He scanned the list and pushed the button for a classic Finnish folk tune, "Hobo's Rose."

"Are you serious?"

"Of course. I'm a hobo and you're a rose."

"I don't feel like dancing."

"Something slower?"

"Not today. Sorry to be a bore. Just not in the mood...maybe I shouldn't have come...all I can think about is work..."

"Join the club," said Jansson.

"You mind if we eat?" said Huusko.

"No."

"I've got terrible table manners."

"Doesn't bother me. I'm sure I've seen worse."

Huusko ordered a pepper steak and cheese potatoes. Jansson chose chicken and rice.

The chicken was dry and the steak tough. The knives were dull and Huusko had to struggle to get a bite-size chunk off the steak.

"Not exactly gourmet cooking?" she said.

"I guess it's sort of like meat."

"I'm on a diet anyway," said Jansson.

Huusko mangled the steak.

"Guess what W.C. Fields said to the waiter in this situation?"

"What?"

"How much for this insult?"

The woman laughed. "Guess what I say in this situation?"

"You gotta go."

"Bingo."

She took her jacket, stood up, shook Jansson's hand and nodded at Huusko.

"Don't stay up too late."

"We won't," Jansson promised.

Huusko watched her swaying hips as she walked away.

"That's that."

# 3.

Nygren was wearing sunglasses. In his long, open overcoat, he resembled an Italian multimillionaire whose silken sheets had entwined the better part of the Italian Riviera's most beautiful women.

"You wanna drive?" asked Raid.

"I'll let you drive for now."

Nygren opted for the back seat again, settling in diagonally with one leg draped across the seat.

"I promised to tell the tale of this car," said Nygren, patting the front seat backrest.

It seemed to Raid that Nygren had read his thoughts.

"If you'd like to hear it."

"Sure."

"Well, the original owner was a popular tango singer back in the early seventies. Died by drowning in his swimming pool around 1975. He had a red brick house with a flat roof, the kind with chinchilla fur on the toilet lid and mink pelts for toilet paper."

"I think I've been there before," said Raid.

"Was there a bar made of birch burl?"

"Something like that."

"Then you know what I'm talking about. His wife sold the house and the other belongings and moved to

Greece to carouse with the local boytoys. The car was purchased by an inconspicuously wealthy farmer from Turku."

"Inconspicuously wealthy?"

"The type that goes around in a ragged sweatshirt and rubber boots patched up with inner tubes even though his bank accounts amount to millions and he has a suitcase of stock certificates under his cot. There's a few of these types at every auction. The more trouble someone else is in, the more likely you are to find them. Then, out of the goodness of their hearts, they offer to buy your half-a-million-euro house for a hundred and fifty grand. You know the type?"

"Yeah."

"Of course, they're always stingy Scrooges. They tear up old newspapers for toilet paper, unless they can get a truckload of the stuff from a bankruptcy estate. If they have a party they might take out a roll, but they always ration everyone to one sheet per wipe."

Nygren lit his cigarette.

Raid's own first car was a Volvo Amazon. A red two-door with a two-liter B20 engine. He had dumped over ten thousand Swedish kronor from his earnings at a chocolate factory into the purchase. Still, the car had been worth every krona.

He had driven it around his first summer vacation in Finland after moving to Sweden. The only downside was that the car still had Swedish plates, so at every stop someone peed on the tires or shouted profanities at him.

Raid glanced in the rear-view mirror. A blue Toyota van had been on their tail for a half hour now.

Some time ago, the van had slowed down and nearly vanished from view, but now it was driving the same speed as they, not quite a hundred yards behind.

"You have something against the inconspicuously wealthy?" Raid asked.

"You noticed? As a guy who's broken every one of God's commandments, I don't have many qualities to brag about, but thank heaven I'm not stingy or all that greedy, though others might have a different opinion. These phony bums convince themselves and everyone else that they aren't really stingy; they just claim to dislike spending. Truth is, they like it immensely—they just love money more than things. They'd wear gold-mesh underwear if it was a gift. Gets on my nerves when they try to squeeze diamonds out of shit. Do you have a gun handy, by the way?"

Nygren's question was jolting, though it flowed naturally within his discourse.

"Just happened to spot one of the shitheads about a hundred yards back."

"I doubt we'll need a gun," Raid said.

"They might be stupid, but they're still dangerous. At least that Sariola. The prison doc said he's some kind of psychopath. For once the doc might be right."

"What was his assessment of you?"

"The prison doc's? Manic-depressive...but otherwise a nice guy."

Nygren craned his neck back as he peered out the rear window.

"How'd they find us?" Raid asked.

"In this car, it's tough to go unnoticed. They probably spotted us in Turku."

"Maybe we should stop and clear things up."

"They don't need any clarification. They want money."

"There was no disagreement over their split?"

"Nope. They got more than they deserved."

"Then let's make it even more clear."

A billboard on the side of the road advertised a service station about a mile up where they could get a donut and coffee for one euro.

"Let's go for coffee and donuts. My treat," said Raid.

Apparently, the special offer hadn't worked, as the parking lot was vacant.

Raid stepped out of the car, stretched his arms and headed toward the station. Nygren paused to look back for a moment before following.

For lack of anything better to do, the balding fifty-something owner had arranged the donuts in a cone-shaped stack. When Raid spoiled the symmetry by buying two donuts, the owner promptly fetched two more from the kitchen to fill in the space.

Raid carried the tray to a corner table while Nygren stood in the doorway watching the parking lot. The blue van paused at the bottom of the exit ramp leading to the station, then turned onto it. Nygren came to the table and started unwrapping sugar cubes, all the while staring out the window. His fingers were as deft as a card-dealer's.

Two men got out of the van, one short and stout, the other average in height, but lean. The skinny one hadn't shaken off his prison look. He wore track pants, running shoes, a leather jacket over a hooded sweatshirt, and long hair combed straight back past the nape of his neck. The short one was dressed in black pressed pants and a brown leather jacket. In his attempt to look like a proper citizen, he ended up looking like a cross between an auto mechanic and a bouncer. The thin man spoke, but the stout one didn't seem to be listening. With a commanding air and determined stride, he started off toward the station.

"The guy in front is the one to look out for—Sariola. Lehto just chauffeurs and packs the heat, but he doesn't use it—he's nothing without Sariola."

Just inside the door, the stout one paused and let his eyes roam the room. His gaze fell on Nygren and a feigned smile spread across his face. He walked over to the table and went through some rendition of "it's a small world."

"Somebody told me they saw you, but I didn't believe him. I thought, well there's plenty of Benzes in the world. What a coincidence! We were just talking about you yesterday, wondering what you're up to nowadays."

He turned to his skinny partner.

"Cream and three sugar cubes…and a donut."

The skinny guy scurried off to the counter and started clinking dishes. The division of labor between the two was plainly evident.

"So what's new?" the stout one said.

"I'm retired."

"Nice that you can afford that."

"Even with a small salary, you put a little away and it starts to build up."

"I reckon you've built up more than just a little."

"Enough for me. I'm a modest man."

"Enough to spare a little for old friends?"

"I'm not a bank."

"And what if you just gave it…for old-time's sake?"

"Here's what I'll give you: some good advice. Drink your coffee, eat your donuts and be on your way."

Shorty dispensed with the cheerful expression.

"Shame. You oughta be thanking us for your little nest egg."

"You should've saved your own cut."

"Not everyone can be as lucky as you."

"It's not about luck, it's about brains. Even if I handed you my last euro, you'd be broke within a week. It's a law of nature. Whosoever hath, to him shall be given."

"Fucking harsh words," the stout one hissed.

As Slim returned to the table with a tray, Shorty took Nygren's insult as an opportunity to twist things back in his favor.

"That hurts... But we're old friends, right? I'm willing to overlook it for a little start-up capital...so little it's almost embarrassing."

"We're launching a business," said slim. "Another guy wants to partner with us..."

The stout one shut him up with a scowl.

"Let's just say fifteen grand," he ventured hopefully.

"Let's not."

The stout one pulled his coat aside to reveal a gun in his shoulder holster.

"If I were you, I'd strike a deal. Afterwards, we can all quietly go our own ways. You remember Lehtinen? He crossed me and didn't want to reconcile. Things didn't go well for him—got a screwdriver in the gut."

"A Phillips," added slim.

The owner slipped quietly behind the cover of the bar.

Nygren patted Raid on the shoulder.

"My nephew isn't fond of guns. If I were you, I'd leave before he gets angry."

The stout one smiled doubtfully, drew his gun and pointed it at Raid's forehead.

"So your nephew's gonna get mad? If I were you, I'd be worried about me getting mad."

Glancing over to see Nygren's reaction was a mistake.

Raid sprang into action, and in a flash, he had the stout one's gun in his hand. Shorty's reflexes were sluggish and his finger grasped at the trigger, but the gun was already gone.

Raid swept out Slim's legs from beneath him and he crashed to the ground beneath his tray of coffee and donuts. In the same instant, Raid swung his gun hand around and thumped the stout one behind the ear with the butt of the pistol. The man sank to his knees and struggled to stay upright.

Raid took a pot of coffee off the counter. The owner cowered behind the donut pile, apparently fearful that his meticulously built tower might collapse.

Raid approached Shorty, kicked him onto his back and emptied the coffee pot onto his crotch.

"You wanted it black, right?"

The man screamed, threw his hands over his crotch and tried to scramble to his feet, but his floundering halted when Raid's knee rammed into his forehead.

Nygren was more merciful. He took a carton of milk from the refrigerator and poured it onto the man's coffee-soaked pants.

Slim crawled toward the exit, leaving a trail of sugar and jam. Raid intercepted him and tore the car keys out of his pocket. Then he bent down and shook him by the hair.

"If we meet again, I promise it won't be pleasant."

He hit him on the right cheek first, then the left. The man's eyes started to roll back.

"That's enough."

Raid eased up and let go. He followed Nygren outside, hurled the keys into a thicket behind the station, and the gun even further.

Nygren sat in the front seat for a change. He looked somber.

"Less would've probably been enough."

"I doubt it."

"Roasted nuts. That's gotta hurt like hell."

"Better his nuts than his soul."

"Sariola's the vengeful type. He won't stop chasing me."

"Maybe so, but at least he'll move a little slower."

"Next time he'll play it safe, which makes him more dangerous. He'll know to be more careful now."

Whatever the case, Nygren knew he owed Raid a debt of gratitude.

"Well done, though. I suppose I made the right choice."

"I suppose so."

* * *

The police were waiting for them about ten miles from the gas station. The cruiser was parked at a bus stop with its blue lights flashing. On both sides of the road were open fields of plowed clay-heavy soil. A tractor was turning over a fresh row with a flock of screaming gulls close behind. Two officers were standing in front of the squad car. One was holding a small stop-sign in his hand, which quickly rose when the Mercedes came into view.

Nygren's face darkened.

"I should have guessed. Where's the gun?"

"It'll turn up when we need it."

Raid snapped on his right blinker and stopped about fifteen feet from the cruiser. The cops stood at the ready, their right hands resting on the butts of their guns.

One of the officers was young, the other a seasoned cop about twenty years older.

The younger one approached the car while the other hung back. The lessons from the police academy had stuck. Raid pushed a button, and with a soft hum, the window slid down.

"License and registration," said the officer.

Raid handed over his driver's license. The cop looked it over, comparing the photo to the live model.

"Registration too."

Raid handed over the Mercedes' registration. The younger officer gave the documents to his partner, who sat down in the cruiser to call them in.

"Out of the car."

Raid and Nygren obeyed.

"Were you guys at the Ellu gas station about fifteen minutes ago?"

Nygren perched his sunglasses on his forehead.

"Not sure if it was Ellu, but some station at any rate. What's going on?"

"What happened over there?"

"We had coffee and donuts. Bargain price."

"There was no incident?"

Nygren shook his head.

"We got a call about a fight and heard somebody pulled a gun. The guys from the neighboring station are over there and said somebody had to be taken to the hospital for burns."

"Sounds awful," said Nygren. "I burned my own ass on the sauna stove once when I was drunk."

The other officer chimed in.

"They'll be here soon."

"The description of the car matches this one. Don't see older Benzes like this every day. Why don't you put your hands on the car and spread your legs."

The younger officer checked both Raid and Nygren, but found nothing.

He pulled his partner aside and they exchanged a few words before returning.

"Alright with you if we search the car?" asked the younger one.

"Wouldn't that call for a search warrant?"

"Not if we suspect you have a radar detector."

"Do you?"

The officers glanced at one another. The older one shook his head, but the younger one took a harder tack. He drew a pair of thin white gloves from his pocket and fanned out his fingers like a magician preparing for a card trick.

"Yes, we do. Open the trunk."

Raid opened it.

The younger officer leaned in and lifted Nygren's suitcase out onto the pavement.

He rummaged through the spare tire compartment and a toolbox. Then he circled around to root through the cabin, glovebox and under the seats. After finding nothing, he turned his attention to the suitcase.

"Just dirty socks and underwear in there," Nygren warned.

The cop didn't believe him and spilled the contents onto the pavement.

"Where you guys headed?" asked the older officer.

"To Lapland, to see the leaves," said Nygren.

"With what gear?"

"The colors look just as nice from a restaurant window, and the trip from the cabin to the restaurant is enough hiking for us."

Just then, the officers from the neighboring station pulled up. A blue and white police van stopped behind the other two cars and two cops in coveralls hopped out. One of them slid open the side door and jerked out a reluctant-looking Lehto, his shirt collar still splattered with jam and sugar crystals.

"These guys look familiar? They the ones that scalded your friend?" asked one of the cops in overalls.

Lehto peered over at Nygren and Raid.

"I already told you my friend knocked over the coffee pot by accident. These guys might have been there, but they didn't do anything."

"You sure about that?"

"Yes."

"The station owner had a very different story. Why would he lie?"

"Maybe he scarfed down too many jelly donuts," Nygren volunteered.

"The guy's whacked," agreed Lehto.

"So you don't know these guys?"

"Complete strangers."

Lehto looked Raid over once more, pretending to search his memory.

"That one looks familiar, but that's just 'cause he looks like my second cousin. Same chin and nose."

The younger officer stared at Raid.

The older cop smiled, but said nothing.

"And you? You speak?"

"When the time is right."

"Now's the time."

"I'm sure I'd remember if I'd met him before. Can't forget a face that stupid."

"I'll second that," said Nygren.

The younger cop started to get skittish and he pulled Lehto in front of himself.

"He might be stupid, but we sure aren't. Both this guy and his buddy with the burns on his nuts are former felons; we've confirmed that. You guys look like the same sort, frankly. I can tell just by looking at you."

"Appearances can deceive," said Nygren.

The cop jostled Lehto.

"You guys fighting over money? Someone get bilked?"

"What's a former felon? What does 'bilk' mean?" Lehto asked, his expression admirably oblivious.

"Don't give me that."

Lehto gazed off toward the shore where a storm front was rolling in.

"Looks like rain."

"Maybe we should bring the whole posse downtown."

"What posse?" said Lehto.

The younger officer could feel the situation slipping through his fingers. This only angered him more and he shook Lehto all the harder. His partner stepped in and clapped a hand on his shoulder.

"That's enough."

"I'll say. Go ask my friend what happened back there before you start accusing people. *He's* the one in the hospital."

One officer escorted Lehto back to the van and the others gathered at a distance to discuss. One of them made a call on his cell phone while the others looked on.

Nygren approached the group.

"How long do we have to wait? It's getting cold out here."

"You can wait in the car. Won't be long."

Nygren and Raid sat down in the car.

"Where's the gun?" Nygren muttered from the corner of his mouth.

"What gun?"

Further down the road, more flashing blue lights came into view. The weary cops were suddenly revived.

"Could've seen this coming," said Nygren.

"Right."

A third squad car, this one a Ford wagon, joined the other two.

The driver opened the liftgate and out hopped a scruffy-looking German shepherd. One of its ears was folded over and it had a mild look in its eyes.

Nygren and Raid knew the drill and stepped out of the car.

The dog sniffed Nygren first, then Raid, but found

nothing interesting. The officer brought the dog over to the Mercedes and opened the door.

"Hopefully you've trimmed his nails," said Nygren. "Leather repair costs a fortune."

The dog sniffed through the rear seating area, then the front. The cop opened the trunk and the dog hopped inside.

"Open the hood."

Nygren pulled the hood latch in the driver's side footwell, then reached under the hood and released the catch. The powerful motor and its trimmings completely filled the engine compartment.

The dog rose up on its hind legs, leaned against the wheel well, and craned its snout toward the engine. It circled round to the other side, but soon its enthusiasm waned and it lowered itself, returned to its handler's side and sat at his feet. The officer patted the dog on the head and offered it a small treat.

He shook his head at the other officers.

The younger officer came over to the Mercedes with a sullen look.

"Get the fuck outta here while you still can."

# 4.

When Lieutenant Kempas took charge of the Helsinki undercover unit, it seemed to be by genetic design. Curious to the core, he took interest in every crumb of intelligence, and he never forgot even the smallest detail. He was diligent, a good judge of character, cunning and brave. Furthermore, he had plenty of impudence with a pinch of well-hidden humanism.

Tall and thin, he stood so ramrod straight that he always seemed to be falling backward. His hair was the color of a dirt road, and was combed straight back from his broad, furrowed brow. The tops of his cheeks were deeply scarred by acne, which had struck at a time when good skin and healthy teeth were just a lot of fuss from city folks. In his case, the nearest pharmacy had been too far away.

There was something vaguely Native American about his appearance. He often stood with his arms crossed over his chest, surly, like the last surviving Apache, his land lost to the white man.

His outfit consisted of black slacks, a burgundy wool coat and a light-blue collared shirt. His tie was navy blue. Overall, his appearance was very neat, but upon closer inspection, tiny balls of lint were visible on his wool coat, two buttons had been sewn on with different colored thread and his tie had a grease stain.

For Kempas, this outfit was unusually casual, almost Bohemian. Ordinarily, he dressed in suits, the origins of which were the subject of plenty of gossip.

The fact that, at fifty years old, he was still a mere lieutenant was due only to Kempas' abrasiveness. He lacked the ability to put himself in his superiors' position, and in any given situation, he did as he saw fit without asking for permission or direction.

While working in the theft unit one year, he had exceeded his budget by a factor of three. Among the expenditures was a helicopter ride worth ten thousand euros.

Despite impressive conviction rates and favorable newspaper articles, his career was at a standstill. Nobody could imagine what he would have done as chief of the department. Helsinki was too small and poor a city for men of large ideas and the balls to execute them. Men who, if the standard-issue 9mm wouldn't do, would gladly take up a bazooka instead.

Every police department in the world had at least one Kempas, but two of his kind was one too many.

Kempas gazed out the window into the yard. A group of gypsies—three men, two women and two children—were filing out of the courthouse. In no apparent hurry, they seemed to be basking in the warm autumn sun.

Kempas felt he'd been given a heavier burden to carry in life, and a gloomier fate than most. He had always taken responsibility for others, which, though it chafed at him, he accepted. Some were weaker than others.

The gypsies stopped next to a battered van. One of the men opened the door and the women and children climbed inside. The men leaned against the van to chat. Each of them had a short black leather coat over a sweater and straight blue pants. All had flawless white collared shirts. The men's idleness was so natural that they seemed almost to be enjoying an evening around a campfire.

Kempas recalled a funny gypsy joke, but he suppressed his amusement.

Sergeant Leino and Officer Lunden, sitting along the wall, glanced at one another.

"Ten after. What's taking her?" wondered Leino.

A knock came at the door and Officer Sanna Susisaari stepped in. Kempas eyed her harshly. Susisaari's blue-grey suit coat had a silver tiepin with a star-shaped Mercedes emblem, which she had received as a gift from Jansson. In Kempas' view, a Mercedes was unfit for police work, as were all other luxury vehicles. An Opel was more appropriate: not too showy, nor too shabby, and perfectly ordinary.

"You made it after all."

"I did."

Since no seats remained in the office, Lunden stood up, and without ceremony, she took his spot.

"A fine collection," she said, attempting to placate Kempas.

On the wall, over a hundred police patches were neatly arranged behind two panes of glass. The collection was the largest at the station and Kempas was plainly proud of it.

The praise worked immediately, and Kempas' expression softened.

"We're interested in the hit man who was a suspect in the Imatra Castle Hotel and warehouse shootings. You, Jansson and Huusko were involved in the investigation."

"You're talking about Raid?"

"Isn't that what they call him?"

"Jansson knows him best... He's in physical rehab, but you can give him a ring."

"We know that. This Raid has been parading around Finland with an old con-man and thief by the name of Nygren. I want to know what they're up to. I doubt they're together for the sake of sightseeing."

"I didn't know Raid was back in Finland, and I don't think Jansson knows either. He would have told me."

"You must know *something*."

The familiar gruffness returned to Kempas' voice. His greatest weakness was his non-existent sense of humor and his inability to distinguish nuance. He was unable to soften his words with humor and often offended others unintentionally.

An astute female subordinate had observed two other major weaknesses besides his dysfunctional sense of humor.

Kempas was a conspiracy theorist. He believed that minorities, like homosexuals, Jews, gypsies, the Sami and the Swedish-speaking Finns, to name a few, formed cliques to benefit themselves at the expense of others. These groups were tacitly conspiring to undermine his work.

The homosexuals, Jewish intellectuals and the Swedish-speaking Finns in government coddled criminals by granting early releases, and he was forced to play dog catcher, trying to cart every last one of them back to the pound. Though he ran himself ragged, more than a few mutts always got away.

Kempas once had a nightmare that hundreds of sprightly little gypsy children had rained down from the sky, and immediately upon landing, they scampered about causing all kinds of mischief. But for every one he caught, a fresh batch of sneering faces appeared.

While in the sauna at a seminar on white-collar crime, having drunk a few beers and several shots, he had divulged the nightmare to some co-workers. They could barely breathe from laughing until they realized the dream was based on a genuine fear.

His other weakness was that he was blind to his own weaknesses. He couldn't be brought to admit a single flaw, even if his own nose hairs were plucked out one by one with a needle-nose pliers.

Still, his subordinates liked him. His unit included some of the Helsinki PD's most sought after positions. He was one of the entire department's best investigators, and unlike many other supervisors, he supported his team even when they messed up. He never let the blame trickle down.

Furthermore, Kempas genuinely cared about his subordinates. He was familiar with each of their life situations, and whether concerning a car purchase or a marriage, he gave stiff but helpful advice. No one on Kempas' team could have a child, a birthday or get married without his knowing it.

His team also appreciated the fact that Kempas encouraged fieldwork. He had no objection if his subordinates spent their evenings at bars frequented by criminals. Much to the contrary, if someone was spending too much time at their desk, Kempas would have a chat with them.

Rumor had it that Kempas had chewed out an

officer for wearing orthopedic sandals to work. In Kempas' opinion, orthopedic footwear was suited for clerks and stewardesses fearful of varicose veins. Certainly not for cops, who should always be ready to wade through mud and shit.

Kempas sat down behind his desk and waited for Susisaari's answer.

"Actually, I don't know anything. Call Jansson," she replied.

"Why do you think Raid's back in Finland?"

"If he's with Nygren, then he's protecting him. I can't think of any other reason. And Nygren would have to be pretty afraid to turn to a guy like Raid."

"Hasn't Raid lived in Sweden for a while?"

"Fifteen years. Jansson's got a whole binder on that. He got the files from the Swedish police."

"Nygren lived there for a few years too, and spent time in jail there. Maybe that's where they met?"

"Maybe."

"Is Raid as dangerous as they say?"

"Based on Jansson's stories, yes. But he's no psycho killer. He'll do what Nygren pays him to do as well as he's capable, and he's capable of a lot."

"Something's not right. Nygren's mostly a con-man, but he knows how to take care of himself. He's never needed a bodyguard before. Now they're going around like two cheeks on the same ass."

Kempas made no attempt to hide his displeasure. He knit his eyebrows and forehead till his face was a sea of knots. His gray eyes flashed angrily from beneath his bushy brows.

In bold strokes, he scratched out strange patterns on the notepad in front of him, practically assaulting the pad with his pen.

Sergeant Leino tried to steal a glance at the pad, but only managed to glimpse a blackened sawblade pattern and a drawing that resembled a toy car. Kempas flipped the pad over. He didn't like to show his cards to friends any more than enemies. The more knowledge he had, the more powerful he was; and the less others had, the weaker they were. For Kempas, that was the pinnacle of philosophy.

"I've known Nygren for over twenty years. He was the first big crook I ever bagged. Back then, I was just a street cop and celebrated it for three days. The next time I nabbed him was ten years ago and now he's out laughing at us again. He won't laugh long."

It seemed to Susisaari that Kempas was taking the matter too personally. The police should loathe crime and wrongdoing, not the criminal.

Susisaari had been involved in several chilling murder investigations, which the news media had portrayed as monstrous. In each case, the perpetrator was caught, and they always seemed like people, not monsters.

Susisaari often recalled a lecture she had attended at the police academy, held by an experienced homicide detective. The lecturer had reminded them that every murderer was someone's child, someone's son or daughter. They didn't have to accept the crime, but they did have to try to understand it. That understanding helped them solve other crimes.

Leino seized his chance to speak.

"We've chatted with Nygren's friends—nobody knows anything. The only thing we can do is follow the two of them and see what they're up to. Every department in the country has been alerted. They'll keep us up to date."

"Up to date on what? That Nygren was doing sixty in his Benz down the straights of Highway 5 and he wears size forty-three Mexican boots? We wouldn't get far on that. I want intel with a capital 'I.' That means wiretaps, surveillance and mindreading if you can figure it out. Whatever it takes to keep him from getting away with something."

Leino and Lunden glanced at one another, then simultaneously at Kempas. The man could get worked up sometimes, but he seemed to be in a frenzy over Nygren.

"It's a little tough to tap his phone when he's on the road all the time."

"He's gotta sleep somewhere. Try to anticipate their route. He's got expensive tastes. Always stays at the best hotel in the area. Put a microphone to the wall and tape their discussions. Go through his cellphone records, too. The calls will tip us off on where they're headed. And try to find out if he has any friends along the way. I know he's got a daughter somewhere around Kuopio and an ex-wife somewhere."

Kempas fidgeted, his body buzzing with excess energy.

"You still need me for anything?" asked Susisaari.

"Get me Jansson's binder on Raid."

"There's not much there, and I doubt what we have would be very useful."

"Someone told me Jansson and Raid are friends."

"Someone's wrong."

"Can't you at least find out how Raid and Nygren know each other?"

Susisaari swallowed "at least" with a straight face.

"I can put in a call to Sweden."

"He has cancer," said Officer Lunden, having waited for just the right moment to drop this bit of information.

"Raid?" Kempas asked.

"Nygren."

"So what?"

"If the guy's dying, why would he be planning another gig? Rumor has it he's got at least a million stashed away from past jobs. That's enough to get him all the way to judgment day."

Kempas weighed Lunden's argument and accepted it, but with reservations.

"If we added up all the cash these crooks would need stashed away, even Nokia's executive stock options wouldn't be enough. Everyone talks about millions, even if all they stole were lollipops. A crook is a crook solely because he has no moderation when it comes to money. He blows it all, and when the money's gone, he does another job. Nygren's no exception, no matter what kind of big shot he's supposed to be. It's a retirement job. Say what you will. He's planning a retirement job."

Lunden objected, though he knew Kempas disliked objections when he was chomping at the bit.

"All the cops ever recovered from the Stockholm bank robbery was about a hundred thousand kronor. They got away with almost six million. And that armored truck in Helsinki netted almost half a million euros. Nygren was behind both of those. He doesn't gamble anymore, doesn't do drugs or drink too much. Sounds plausible that he'd have money stashed away."

"Has this cancer claim been verified?"

"The doctor is sticking to patient confidentiality, but it's been supported by other accounts. The tumor is malignant."

"What about Lehto and Sariola? They just bumped into Nygren by accident? They used to work together, you know."

"According to our sources, they got into a fight," said Lunden.

Kempas was innately distrustful.

"A bluff?"

"Sariola ended up in the hospital with scalding hot coffee on his nuts. The burns sure weren't bluffing. According to the station owner, it was about money. Sariola was demanding cash and Nygren wouldn't pay. So Sariola threatened Nygren with a gun and Raid flattened him."

"Isn't that enough reason in itself to have Raid along?" said Susisaari. "Nygren has bread and his old cronies want a piece of it."

"Nygren's done fine on his own before. And brains are always better than brawn."

Unable to sit still, Kempas strode over to the window. The gypsy family was still flocked around the old van. One of the men was sitting behind the wheel. The women were in the rear and the children were playing on a nearby sidewalk. Kempas concluded that one of their entourage must be awaiting a sentencing in the courthouse. Tight-knit family as they were, they were loath to leave one of their own behind.

"You two can devote all your time to Nygren, but I don't want any overtime filed. If you need to hound him across the countryside, that's fine; do whatever you deem necessary. And feel free to spend the night in a hotel, but three stars max."

Susisaari got up.

"I doubt you'll have any use for me anymore."

Kempas was so preoccupied he hardly noticed her departure.

"Can we use the helicopter?" asked Leino.

Kempas shot a look at Leino, who immediately regretted the joke. Then a smile spread over Kempas' face.

"Sure…as long as I can ride along."

# 5.

"This the one?" Raid asked, stopping next to a chain-link fence. A sign on the fence read: Mara's Auto Inc.—Plain Honest Car Sales Since 1998."

Behind the fence were a couple dozen cars and a large camper. No customers were in sight, but somebody was in the camper.

"The day I find an honest car salesman, they'll have Mardi Gras in heaven."

Nygren pried himself out of the car and lit a cigarette.

"Let's do it."

Raid closed the fence gate and flipped the sign over so it read, "Closed." The door to the building opened and a man dressed in a designer sweater and pressed pants stepped outside. The man was over fifty years old and portly. His thin, greasy hair was combed with mathematical precision over as much of his bald spot as possible, and he was smoking a ragged cigar. His other hand fiddled with a ring of keys in his pocket. Raid could hear the keys jingling.

"The one and only Mara," said Nygren.

"The one and only Nygren. I was wondering who's this yuppie shutting my gate, but…"

"Just came to do some inventory."

A couple of years of honest car sales taught more about reading faces and gestures than ten years at a university. Mara looked at them with the same couldn't-care-less look that he used to soften up customers wanting to trade in old cars.

"Inventory?"

Further back, two men in black leather jackets stepped out onto the porch.

"Three salesmen and not a single customer. No wonder the place isn't pulling a profit."

"Just a couple friends who dropped by to say hello."

Nygren glanced at the men. They didn't look like anybody's friends.

Mara tried to manage a friendly smirk, but the attempt fell flat.

"Good timing. Just made coffee…"

Nygren peeked inside a BMW 740 parked next to the building. "A hundred thousand miles, and of that, fifty thousand driven backwards. Otherwise the odometer would say one fifty, right?"

"Phhh. That's my own car."

"Mara here's notorious for the fact that whenever a car comes in the front gate, fifty-thousand miles go out."

"What if the car's been driven less than fifty?" Raid asked.

"Then the buyer gets free miles—a car that's been driven less than zero miles."

Mara's friendly face started to fade.

"Can I help you guys with something? Pretty busy here…"

Nygren scanned the empty lot.

"Looks like it. Didn't you get word?"

"I heard something from the boys, but I didn't quite follow your reasoning."

"What's so complicated about it?"

"They said you want a hundred grand, but they must have heard you wrong. I ain't got that kinda money. Lucky if I can afford coffee and a few biscuits."

Mara's buddies chuckled.

Nygren held out his hand.

"The money."

"You really expect to traipse outta here with a hundred grand?" Mara's belly shook as he laughed.

"That's right."

Mara glanced back and the goons in leather stepped forward.

"What's this inventory you're talking about?" asked Mara.

"Perhaps it's best if I put it in proper Finnish: cough up the fucking money or die."

Nygren's sudden anger startled Mara, and he stepped back, but his leathered backup calmed his nerves.

"There must be some mistake here, my friend."

"Correct. You're gravely mistaken if you think I'll buy the same bullshit as your customers."

"Sorry, but business suffers from too much standing around. You should go now."

With a nod, Mara stepped aside and the leathered pair advanced on Nygren.

Unfazed, Nygren stood his ground, and the men seemed to hesitate.

"I suggest you go quietly," said one of them as he reached for Nygren's arm. Suddenly, the thug screamed and jerked his hand away. Raid stepped between the two of them brandishing a heavy tire iron.

"That hurt?" said Nygren. "Pity."

The other tough backed away, rummaging for something in his pocket. Raid slammed the iron down on his collar bone, snapping it. The pain was so intense that he dropped to his knees howling.

Mara could see the situation was getting out of control, and despite his excess weight, he quickly waddled off toward the camper.

Raid lifted a gas can out of the trunk of Nygren's Mercedes and doused the front of the camper with it. Mara peered out from behind the curtains, his eyes darting wildly.

Nygren knocked on the door of the camper.

"Call the fire department. Something's burning here."

He flicked a match at the wall and the camper burst into flames.

Mara gestured frantically behind the window.

"There's a propane tank in here… It's gonna blow!"

"Thanks for the heads up. We'll back up a little and watch. Always wanted to see what one of those does when it blows."

Mara's lackeys watched the blaze apathetically as Raid wagged his gun at them.

"Stay put."

Raid got Nygren's Mercedes, backed it up till it was ten feet from the camper door, and opened the trunk.

The flames spread quickly, engulfing the entire camper. Thick, black smoke billowed off the smoldering fiberglass shell. A window on the camper shattered with a bang, and a panicked voice could be heard from inside.

"I'm burning in here... This is murder! You hear me, Nygren? Murder!"

"Murder indeed," Nygren said casually.

"I'm coming out!"

Mara tried to open the door, but Raid pushed it closed and Nygren helped him wedge it with a chunk of two-by-four. Panic-stricken, Mara peeked out the window to see what was blocking the door.

"Take it out... My clothes are smoking... I'm burning..."

"No, you aren't. There must be some mistake."

One of the henchmen tried to slip away, but Raid stopped him with a wave of his gun. The man froze mid-creep.

"I'll give you twenty grand now and the rest later!" Mara shouted, his offer broken by sobs.

Nygren waited a moment longer. From inside, he could hear pounding and bellowing. Mara was trying to bash down the door with every one of his three hundred and thirty pounds. Nygren kicked out the two-by-four and Mara came crashing through the door. Raid gave him an extra boost of speed and the smoldering man plowed headlong into the trunk of the Mercedes. Raid slammed it shut.

Nygren poured what was left of the gas can onto and inside of Mara's BMW. With relish, he struck the match. The two henchmen put their fingers in their ears.

Nygren tossed the match onto the hood of the car. The gasoline vapors whooshed and the entire car shuddered as flames were sucked inside. In the space of a second, the car was engulfed in a column of fire.

They had barely made it to the road when the camper exploded. The shock wave shot the walls in four different directions and the roof collapsed.

A few hundred yards down the road, the first fire truck went zooming past in the opposite direction. Immediately following it were an ambulance and more fire trucks. Nygren watched as they disappeared in the distance.

"Must be a fire somewhere."

A few miles further, they found an old logging road that led through the remains of a clear-cut pine forest. On the shoulders of the road were huge log piles and bulldozed mounds. The chaff left by mechanical harvesters lay on every side. Raid drove to the end of the road, killed the engine and popped the trunk.

Mara lay in a fetal position, covered in soot, his clothes still smoking.

Nygren slapped him on the back.

"You said something about twenty grand."

Mara sat up with a dazed expression, still rattled by the jolting ride down the logging road and the smoke in his lungs. Nygren settled onto a stump and waited. He surveyed what was left of the peat forest, laid waste by the harvesters.

"It'll be fifty years before this place recovers."

Mara crawled out. His trousers were riddled with burn holes and his boxers were jutting out of the holes.

Nygren looked more interested in his surroundings than in his former business partner.

"Fuck, look at me," Mara muttered.

Nygren turned to look. The sight amused him.

"You can knock the cost of your pants off your

debt, call it fourteen euros."

Mara took a breath of the fresh forest air and started to come to his senses. A cellphone in his hip pouch started to play a polka.

Raid snatched the phone and bashed it against a rock. The polka abruptly cut short.

"The money's at my place... In the garage..."

"Let's go get it," Nygren said.

They led Mara into the front-passenger seat and Nygren slid in behind him. Raid drove.

Nygren stared gloomily at the back of Mara's head.

"What makes shitheads like you so greedy? Why don't you enlighten us to pass the time?"

Mara sulked silently.

"I give you startup capital and the opportunity to make some money. You thank me by trying to rip me off. Then you hire a couple of goons so you don't have to cough up a single cent. Were they worth it?"

"I didn't have time...the money was tied up in cars and..."

Nygren slapped Mara on the back of the head.

"You haven't made a single payment in over a year. Don't give me that shit."

"There must be some mistake. My accountant..."

Nygren whacked him again and he fell silent.

"If there's no accounting, there's no accountant either. Save your stories for the tax auditor."

Mara's white-brick house was on the south-facing shore of a lake. The house had at least 3,500 square feet. Nygren surveyed the property.

"So this is how a plain honest car salesman from the heartland of Savo lives."

"It's my wife's house...and the kids'."

"On paper, you mean."

Mara opened the garage door. There was ample space for two cars and a small red sports car was parked in one of the stalls.

"That's my wife's."

Mara's confidence was beginning to return. They'd let him live, he thought.

As Nygren looked him in the eyes, Mara tried to smile to no effect. He endured Nygren's stare for a moment before turning away.

"The instant they look away, you can see right through 'em. Only for about a tenth of a second, but if you're sharp, it's enough."

The door to the house opened and a forty-something woman peeked out. After seeing the shape her husband was in, she hurried to his side.

"What has happened to you? You is alright?" she stammered in a heavy Russian accent.

"We had a little fire," Nygren said calmly.

"Have you been to doctor?"

"Tatjana, go inside. Everything's fine."

She regarded Raid and Nygren with suspicion.

"There is something wrong?"

"No. Go inside."

She wasn't fooled.

"Something is wrong. I call police."

"You fucking will not. Get inside, woman!"

Accustomed to the more Slavic conversational style, she obeyed immediately.

Mara slid the desk aside. Behind it, built into the brick wall, was an opening covered with a piece of particle board. Mara bent down and pulled out a metal box. He put it in his lap and nearly dove inside.

"Twenty thousand even," said Mara as he snapped

the case shut. He tried to squirrel it back into the hole as though all was settled but Nygren snatched it away.

"We're not in that much of a hurry."

The box contained some more money and a black booklet. Nygren briskly counted out the money.

"Another twenty-grand. I'll take that too."

"No, you fucking won't…"

The futility of Mara's words sank in as Nygren leafed through the booklet.

"You seem to be doing pretty well. According to this you have a few hundred grand in Spain. I'll take this as a keepsake. If the rest of the money isn't in my account by the deadline, the tax auditor's gonna have some interesting bathroom reading material."

Mara made an attempt at humility.

"Please, I guarantee you'll get your money…just don't take the ledger. It's no use to you. I use it every day. Some of my cars are on loan, and my debts are in there… I'll give you something extra. You want a new car? What about your friend? I can arrange something…"

"If it weren't for your lousy memory, I might consider it. But you tend to forget those pesky details like paying debts. Anyway, I already have a car."

Nygren slipped the ledger into his pocket.

Mara clenched his teeth, but remained silent.

"You know the account number. We'll be waiting for you to remit the balance."

Mara hurled the empty case into the corner of the garage.

"And don't think you can get out of this by surrounding yourself with more muscle. Until you pay up, every night could be your last. And you can be sure the interest will keep accruing."

Tatjana was waiting in the yard with a worried expression. Once Raid and Nygren were in the car, she made a dash for the garage. Mara came out and roughly shoved her aside.

"The perfect Finnish family. Brick house by the lake. Who could ask for more," Nygren reflected. "Or maybe you could. You can't buy happiness, after all…"

He waved the wad of bills in Raid's face.

"But you sure can try. Over forty thousand. Our plain honest boy from Savo's gonna cry his eyes out over this."

"What about the rest?"

"He wouldn't dare stiff me."

The satisfaction on Nygren's face suddenly vanished, as though wiped away. His eyes became bleary and he clutched at his stomach.

Raid pulled over at a bus stop.

"Think I… Got a little overexcited… Well worth it, though…"

Nygren began to shiver.

"Why's it gotta act up now…"

Raid reclined the passenger seat to a nearly supine position and spread a felt blanket over Nygren.

"I feel better already," he said, though he didn't look it.

"You sure you can manage?"

"Can't stop now… The fun has just begun. Let's stick with the original plan."

# 6.

On Thursday morning, Jansson decided to stay in bed.

They had stayed at the Millhouse Tavern until last call. After Anna's departure, Huusko had turned to the bottle for comfort. The fact that the relationship wasn't going to be revived was finally hitting home for him.

The conversation between Jansson and Huusko had centered around one topic: women. Huusko rattled off his heartaches one by one. He confessed to having changed his attitude toward women after his wife left him when he was recovering from the gunshot.

Jansson had championed the female cause and kept Huusko's generalizations at bay.

As the evening wore on, Huusko had softened up, and when the band finally struck up at nine, he was ready for a new conquest. He focused his efforts on a woman at the neighboring table who turned out to be a Finnish language teacher at the local high school.

In the end, Jansson wound up heading back to the physical rehab center alone. Huusko headed for the woman's nearby home.

The decision to stay in bed had nothing to do with

a hangover. Having only drunk moderately, he felt reasonably alert. He simply had no desire to submit to the hazing of another physical therapist: "Doesn't Jansson's back bend? Jansson, tuck in your belly. Jansson, breathe deeply…"

He was an adult, and known as a deliberate man. He knew how to take care of himself and his body. And even if it wasn't in tip-top shape, it got him where he needed to go.

His final reason for staying in bed rolled in with the weather. The first real fall storm was raging outside. Jansson had opened the window as far as the latch allowed, taken a blanket out of the cabinet, and wrapped it around his shoulders. He enjoyed the gusts of wind as they banked off the window and swept across his face. The light patter of rain on the window sill only increased his pleasure.

Jansson began to doze lightly. He was unruffled by the subconscious knowledge that breakfast was sailing past: an assortment of fish, hard-boiled eggs, low-fat cheese, whole-grain bread, high-fiber muesli, and herbal tea. Jansson disdained all of them.

He felt the same triumphant joy that he had as a child, after exaggerating his ailments to his parents and getting permission to stay home from school. His brother and sisters always stopped by to drop a few jealous comments, but he only burrowed deeper into the softness of his bed. Mom always came to give him a kiss and dad smoothed his hair with his coarse hand.

Then the two went to work at the factory.

His father had occasionally suspected that Jansson would become an everlasting sloth, but becoming a police officer had changed him completely. Jansson had become extremely conscientious. If he were ill with a fever under 102°, he still stumbled into work. For over thirty years, he had taken care of his job without once shirking responsibility. Now, it seemed he could allow himself to take things a little easier again. He didn't have to lie to his mother and father, nor explain to the overzealous therapist. It was enough that he said what he did and didn't want. He wanted to sleep and listen to the wind and rain.

A knock came at the door, and though Jansson heard it, he resolved to ignore it.

"Wake up, it's Huusko!"

Jansson pulled the blanket over his head.

Huusko just thumped harder.

"Everything alright?"

Jansson peeked out from beneath the blanket.

"Yeah."

"You have a hangover?"

"Let me sleep."

"Open the door."

"No."

"You sure everything's alright?"

"Yes. Go away."

"Come on. Let's get some breakfast."

"No."

"What'll I tell 'em?"

"Whatever you want."

"And you'll take the rap for it?"

"Go away!"

Jansson banished Huusko's visit from his mind and sank once again to the verge of sleep.

Over thirty years as a cop with ten more years till retirement, and he was already sick and tired of this line of work. There had been countless mornings when he would have rather stayed in the warmth and comfort of his bed, but had forced himself to get up and go in.

Jansson opened his eyes.

*Why don't you quit then?*

It seemed to Jansson that the question was posed by a second self hiding within—one braver than the first.

But the first wasn't about to cave.

*Grown-ups have to take responsibility. Adults don't give up when it's not fun anymore. Life ain't no joyride. Boredom and suffering are part of the deal.*

*You've already been dealt your share of that.*

This was not Jansson's first such internal battle. Every time he was called to investigate a death at somebody's home, he had fought a similar one. In a city the size of Helsinki, hundreds of deaths with no criminal involvement occurred in homes every year: a middle-aged man goes to bed after reading the newspaper, kisses his wife and rolls over, never to wake again. At least not in this place or time. As he drifts off to sleep, he's oblivious to the fact that he'll never again taste the fresh coffee his wife makes in the mornings, never smell the fresh ink on the daily edition of the *Helsingin Sanomat*. To Jansson, it didn't seem fair. A person should get some kind of final warning, he thought, a chance to settle up with themselves and others.

Just two weeks before coming to physical rehab, Jansson had been the on-duty lieutenant on a particularly quiet evening. To burn some time, he had gone to investigate a body found in an apartment in Töölö. The man had been dead for a couple of days. His son, a college student coming home to visit, had found the body.

Jansson had noticed the name on the door. When he saw the deceased, he recognized him as a friend from high school.

Suddenly he had realized that the ranks of his peers were thinning out. The following morning, he noticed that the first thing he read in the *Helsingin Sanomat* were the obituaries. Huusko claimed that reading the obituaries was a sign of surrender. Once it came to that, he had said, it was time to start shopping for cemetery plots.

Another knock came at the door. Jansson plugged his ears, but this time it was relentless.

"It's Anna. Huusko's worried about you and I promised I'd come have a look…"

Jansson got up and wrapped the blanket around himself. He opened the door a crack. Anna was wearing a white pant suit. Her hair was tied back in a ponytail, lending a somewhat more girlish look than the previous evening.

"Nothing to worry about. Just tired…"

"Can I come in anyway?"

Jansson stepped aside and opened the door. A large mirror hung in the entry and he realized how laughable he looked swaddled in his blanket. A single feather for his head and he might have passed for a balding Indian chief.

Jansson took a seat on the bed and gathered the blanket into his lap. He had a nagging suspicion that he looked no less laughable sitting on the bed with a blanket in his lap.

Anna glanced at the window. The wind was tossing the drapes nearly sideways.

"Can I shut the window?"

"No."

"You wanna freeze to death?"

"Sounds good."

She sat quite naturally on the edge of the bed.

"Feeling a little down, I guess?"

"Just thinking… And I like the wind and rain."

"You should join us… Did I offend you somehow?"

"No."

"Some people don't like to be bossed around, but it's part of my job."

"I suppose so."

"Will you come later?"

"A little later."

"Glad to hear you're not contemplating suicide…"

"Nah. Just in a contemplative mood."

Anna realized she was toying with her ring, and she set her hands firmly in her lap.

"Has Huusko said anything about us?"

"A little."

"We got involved in a relationship while he was recovering from a gunshot wound…"

"You're both adults."

"It wasn't real… I felt pity for him… Close to dying and his wife leaves him… I don't understand women like that…"

"But you… Your relationship helped him."

"It still wasn't smart… My own life was messed up too… Now everything's finally back in order, at least sort of. I wouldn't want to mess it up again…"

"With Huusko?"

"Yeah…and I doubt he's ready for a relationship anyway."

"Best if you're frank with him… Or would you

like me to say something?"

"I'm a grown-up. I have to handle my own problems."

"Same goes for all of us."

"But thanks anyway."

As she gazed at Jansson, her serious expression melted into a smile. Jansson could see why Huusko was obsessed, even if his type was usually younger. Anna had a rare blend of warmth and sexiness.

She was just the type that every young man would love to lose his boyhood to. Without fear, and without guilt.

"Mind telling me what you've been thinking about here all by yourself?" She smiled wryly. "In the blowing wind and pouring rain."

"A boring man's boring personal matters."

"You're not boring, much to the contrary."

"Boring personal matters, then."

"I'd still be interested."

Jansson considered lying, but decided to tell the truth.

"Just wondering how I'll ever make it to retirement when I'm already tired of being a cop."

"I understood from Huusko that police work was your calling."

"It was…and still is sometimes."

"You do important work, you're valued, and you're in a leadership position. For most that would be enough."

"I'm fifty-four. If I ever wanted to do something else, now would be the time."

"Like what?"

"Move to the country and raise chickens. Or to an island in the Gulf of Finland and fish for a living…

Fix up old cars…"

Anna laughed.

"Good choices. But you've got thirty years of work that you enjoy under your belt. That's nothing to sneeze at."

"What about you?"

"I'd have been a pediatrician or an architect… I guess I wasted a lot of time when I should have been soul-searching."

"You have a fine profession."

Anna looked almost bashful when she asked, "And your wife? Would she move to the country with you?"

"Maybe."

"You must be happy together."

"I have a good wife."

"And she certainly has nothing to complain about."

"Well, I'm old, tired and bored."

"I wouldn't say so. Sympathetic and safe, with a good sense of humor. You wouldn't believe how much women appreciate those things."

"That so?"

"You bet. And fifty-four's not so old, at least not for a man. I'm forty-two myself."

"Now that I don't believe," said Jansson.

Anna smiled at his politeness. She took his hand and held it between hers.

"Will you at least come for lunch?"

"I guess so," he shrugged.

"Good."

She rose, but hesitated before leaving.

"You're a good listener… It'd be nice to talk more sometime… Just the two of us."

Anna left, leaving only the scent of her perfume in the room and a restless feeling in Jansson's chest. Was it really just a chat she wanted, or was that a sign that she wanted more?

Over the course of three days, Jansson had noticed that many couples had formed among the men and women at the rehab center. He also knew that some of them had arranged to meet again.

Jansson had been faithful for all thirty-two years of his marriage. As far as he was concerned, his wife hadn't shown adequate appreciation for his faithfulness. Unlike the other women Jansson knew, his wife was nearly devoid of jealousy, so devoid that it sometimes troubled him. Did she think he was unable to attract other women?

Unable to sit still any longer, he stepped into the shower. On his way downstairs, Officer Susisaari called to tell him about Lieutenant Kempas' request.

"I just chatted with him yesterday."

"He wants all the files on Raid. Didn't you have a whole binder on him?" she asked.

"Go ahead and send it. It's filed in the archives."

"You know…Kempas is a good detective and all, but I don't like his style."

"Neither do I. Try to put up with it."

"How's Huusko managing?"

"Huusko manages no matter what."

"Are we talking about the same guy? Detective Hannu Huusko?"

"One and the same."

"Tell him I said hi. You guys are missed over here, even him."

The lounge in the lobby was nearly empty and the veterans' table was deserted. Jansson grabbed the day's edition of the *Helsingin Sanomat* and started to leaf through it. From the lobby, he could see the cafeteria where they were preparing for lunch. The staff was setting piles of food and plates onto the buffet.

A group of women in white terry cloth robes with towels wrapped around their heads was coming from the direction of the swimming pool. Huusko was lagging behind a bit, his arm around a woman in a bikini who was laughing at his banter.

"See you tonight," said Huusko as he cut off in Jansson's direction.

"What's going on tonight?" asked Jansson.

"A dance. Nice to finally see you among the living again. I was afraid I'd have to break down the door."

Jansson marveled at Huusko's carefree manner. He would have expected the setback with Anna to have slowed him down a bit.

"Susisaari called and sends her greetings."

"I'm gonna toss my bag in the room. You're coming to lunch, right?"

"I guess so."

Huusko hurried off to his room. Apparently forgetting that he was a patient at a physical rehab center, he bounded up the stairs by fours.

The war veterans seized their regular table again. Jansson's cellphone rang and he withdrew to a quiet corner.

"It's me."

Jansson recognized the voice immediately.

"Hope it's not a bad time. I heard you were in physical rehab."

"Not a bad time at all. I heard you were in Finland."

"Right."

"Work or play?"

"Tough to say."

"Why?"

"Sometimes it feels like work, sometimes it feels like play."

"What does?"

"You don't know?"

"Yeah. You're on the road with Nygren. Should I know why?"

"Not as a cop."

"You're not up to anything criminal?"

"Not really."

"Not doing anything I wouldn't do?"

"No. Pretty sure you'd approve of everything I'm doing."

"A certain colleague of mine thinks Nygren's planning a big job."

"Not true."

"You sure?"

"Yes."

"Why'd you call, then?"

"I want you guys to leave us alone."

"Hey, I'm just a plain lieutenant—I don't have that kind of sway. Besides, the lieutenant who's after Nygren is a pretty tough nut to crack. Almost impossible."

"You can assure your colleague he's wasting his time. We're attending to fully legitimate matters."

"Have you known Nygren long?"

"Yes."

"You protecting him from someone?"

"Yes again."

"You staying in Finland long?"

"Tough to say."

"Is there a number I can get hold of you at...if I hear something."

"I'll call you."

"Might be better to meet in person."

"Not yet."

"Where you at now?"

"On the road," Raid replied in English.

"On the road," Jansson repeated.

"Right."

# 7.

Raid and Nygren were the only customers at the village general store. The shopkeeper stood behind the meat counter in a white coat, following them with a curious gaze. The little store had been forcibly converted into a crowded mini-mart and the register had been squeezed right in front of the entrance. Behind the register was a woman in her fifties, likely the shopkeeper's wife, judging from her self-important expression. She sat ramrod straight, like a prison guard. Not a single customer would get by her without paying.

Nygren had piled a case of beer, a loaf of bread, cheese, canned pea soup, sausage links, a can of coffee and a couple of cartons of milk into the shopping cart. He lingered in the cookie aisle and picked out some chocolate cookies with strawberry filling, then veered sharply right and stopped in front of the meat counter.

"A half pound of sliced ham."

The shopkeeper took careful aim with his metal tongs and lifted a pile of ham onto some wax paper. The scale showed nine ounces.

"That's fine," said Nygren.

His generosity won the shopkeeper's approval.

"Might I ask if you're the owner of the old Nurminen place?"

Nygren nodded.

"Pleased to meet you. Folks around here sometimes wonder what type of guy owns that place."

"This type."

The shopkeeper glanced at Nygren as conspicuously as he dared. Dressed in sunglasses, a long black Italian coat and handmade Mexican boots, Nygren was certainly not a common sight at the village store. He wasn't a common sight anywhere.

"Not that we're all that nosy out here in the country—it's just nice to know…in case we bump into each other."

"Right."

The shopkeeper could see he wasn't getting any more out of Nygren.

"Anything else I can get you?"

"A couple dozen cabbage rolls."

"Garbage rolls…as they're called around these parts."

The shopkeeper's regional Savo humor got no rise out of Nygren. He remained taciturn.

The cashier studied Nygren's bills as though certain they were forgeries. Nygren glanced at Raid. His background was evidently well known to the townspeople.

"Thank you," said Nygren, looking the cashier directly in the eyes. The woman covered her neck with her hands, seemingly fearful that Nygren might pull a stiletto and part her throat from ear to ear.

The Mercedes climbed a long hill, curving steadily to the right before abruptly reaching the turnoff to Nygren's estate. On the left was a steep bluff and just before the turnoff was a dense birch forest. There were no road signs or mailboxes at the intersection, nor anything else to indicate what lay ahead.

Raid feathered the brakes just enough to make the turn without stopping at the intersection.

The road was pitted and flanked by birches. A slippery layer of leaves had already fallen onto the road.

They passed a barn with corn-crib siding that was listing to one side. At one end of the barn were some farm machines unfamiliar to Raid. On the right, they passed a small yellow wooden house. A woman's bicycle was parked in front of the stairs and smoke rose from the chimney.

"That old lady's almost eighty and still gets by on her own," Nygren said without turning his head. "Some claim she takes the tractor and plows the road by herself."

They approached a turnoff up ahead where a smaller road broke off to the left. Nygren pointed left with his thumb. A sign at the turnoff read: Nurminen.

This side road of a side road went on for a couple of hundred yards and terminated in front of a house on a hill. Thinly scattered birch whips were growing in the driveway, and the apple trees were sprawling and dilapidated. The supports that held up the branches had rotted and snapped, but despite their neglect, the trees were brimming with apples.

The lawn had grown into a tall meadow that was now yellowing and dying.

At the foot of the trees was a garden swing, and beyond that, about ten berry bushes and an overgrown potato field.

Further still was a fallow field that sloped gently toward a lake about two hundred yards away. A few summer cottages were visible on the opposite shore.

The one-and-a-half-story house was large and straight, but just as neglected as its surroundings. The granite foundation was level and solid. White paint was flaking off the walls, revealing the gray surface of the wood. The moldings around the windows were crazed with cracks, but the small window panes were intact.

Behind the house was a large barn with a stone foundation and a shed, which housed what appeared to be a sauna on the opposite end. Next to the wall, an old wood-burning stove with a pile of crumbling sauna rocks had been left out to rust.

If the outbuildings had ever had paint, there was no evidence of it. Still, they stood straight and square.

Nygren looked around with a lordly expression.

"It looks better than I expected. It's been three years since I was here last. I figured the local hooligans would've at least busted the windows for lack of anything better to do."

He fished an old-fashioned key out of a gap in the porch and unlocked the door.

The stench of an abandoned cabin wafted outside. It was one part oblivion, a second part memories, and a third part damp wood and rugs—with a pinch of the scent of cardboard, the same smell you get after opening a cardboard box that has sat in the cellar for years.

Nygren took in the lush aromas.

"We'll have to air it out and put on the heat."

Mice had stormed the cupboard. The counter was

strewn with fallen flour and sugar from the chewed up sacks. Little feet had spread flour all over the table as well. Black droppings the size of rice grains were everywhere.

"And clean up a little."

The cabin was somewhat devoid of furniture. In the kitchen were a small dining table, two spindle-back chairs, wood and electric stoves and a refrigerator. The floral-patterned shades, once yellow and green, were now dusty and sun-bleached.

In the living room were a 1960s hide-a-bed and a bookshelf of the same vintage. There were no books, only a stack of magazines and a few china cups. In addition, there was a rocking chair, a shabby faux-leather recliner and a black-and-white television.

On the window sill were a couple of flowers, now dried to an unrecognizable state. A living room door opened into the bedroom, where a cot lay next to a small nightstand and an electric heater, nothing else. A staircase painted the color of dried blood ascended from the entry to the upstairs.

"A little run-down, but it'll do," said Nygren.

"Pretty old."

"Turn of the century. Timber framed and well built. Not a single spot of rot. An old farm couple used to live here. The husband was a stubborn old mule...looked after the place till he was nearly eighty. The kids moved to Sweden to look for work, and when the folks died, they let the place go downhill. First they sold the fields, then the forests, then the house. It's still got ten acres, though."

Raid looked at the thin sprinkling of furniture.

"You did the interior decorating?"

"I was here for a summer and bought everything I

needed at the flea market. The upstairs is empty."

"You got a story for this place too?"

"A few. I'll tell you sometime."

They heard the rumble of an approaching tractor and Raid glanced out the window. Nygren came to look too.

"Neighbor. Probably saw the car."

"You guys on good terms?"

"Nothing to worry about."

Nygren stepped outside and Raid followed. The tractor plowed through the grove of saplings that had overgrown the drive and stopped just in front of the steps. A man in his sixties swung out of the cab. He was dressed in a sweatsuit that was far too tight and a cap with a plastic bill. On his feet was a pair of rubber boots with leather uppers. Stylistically, the ensemble would be admirably true to form if he was a farmer in the '60s.

The man walked up, his hand stretched out toward Nygren. They shook.

Nygren introduced Raid.

"My boy saw the Benz in town, so I figured my old neighbor had come to visit."

The man nodded toward the house.

"I've been dropping by every now and again to make sure everything's holding up."

"Thanks."

"You figuring to stay a while?"

Nygren shook his head.

"We'll be on our way the day after tomorrow at the latest. We're headed north. This just happened to be on the way."

"So we won't have a new neighbor after all."

"You have time for a drink?"

"We're not so busy out in the country that we don't have time for a little hooch."

He followed Nygren inside.

"You managed to clean up already."

"The mouse shit was everywhere."

"Not sure where they come from, but every time you turn your back…" said the man.

"Whiskey or Cognac?"

"Well, since you're buying… Cognac."

Nygren poured a stiff shot into a water glass.

"Regular glass alright with you?"

"Or straight from the bottle."

Nygren sat down at the table and his neighbor sat across from him.

"I reckon I should mention the couple of snoops I saw here a week ago."

"What kind of snoops?"

"I was coming back from fishing along the lower road one evening… There was a blue van in the road a ways up. Something seemed a bit fishy so I went in closer to have a look. Couple guys peeked in the windows and walked around the house. Pretty sure they looked through the barn, too. I tried to make a lot of noise when I come up, and when they seen me they scurried off to the van and hightailed it."

"How many?" asked Raid.

"Two. I didn't get a close look, but one of 'em was skinny and the other kind of stocky. They seemed to take an interest in everything… Could just be tramps, but still…I thought you oughta know."

"Did you get a look at the plates or what kind of van it was?" asked Raid.

"Some sort of Japanese make... Not real new, but not too old either. Didn't catch the plates. I wasn't really on the ball enough to even think of it. They were in a real hurry to go once they seen me. Probably felt guilty."

"Thanks. Let's have another…" Nygren splashed some more Cognac into the man's glass.

When only a sliver remained in the bottle, the neighbor left. He lurched clumsily into the tractor's cab, gave a rakish wave and weaved off. Nygren stood on the steps and watched him go.

"It pays to be on good terms with the neighbors."

"Sariola and Lehto," said Raid.

"Yep."

"Did they know about this place?"

Nygren took a swig of Cognac.

"My fault. We stopped here briefly before our last gig."

"So they've been dogging you for a while."

"It would seem so."

"Then they'll come here after us."

Nygren had a faraway look. Without a word, he walked to the garden swing, sat down and kicked forcefully until the swing ground into motion.

"A man gets to thinking he's pretty clever. A completely different caliber than the other assholes who take shitty gigs and bounce in and out of the pen. But he drags all these idiots along. Why? Because he has no choice. There's a shortage of qualified staff, and what few there are run their own gigs. In the end, the idiots fuck up and the gig falls flat. That's the way it is and the way it'll always be."

Nygren wasn't angry. Though his words were cross, he sounded almost bored.

"Fortunately, that life is in the past. I don't have to deal with the idiots anymore. We'll leave tomorrow."

"I suggest you take care of your business now, though. Might have to leave in a hurry."

"There's an old shotgun and some ammunition in the attic."

"I'll keep that in mind."

"Follow me," said Nygren.

Raid followed him into the barn, a ramshackle structure about thirty feet long and twenty feet wide. The door was bolted with a sturdy lock made by the village blacksmith.

Inside, it smelled of earth and rotting wood. Part of the floor was dirt and the rest cast concrete. A urine gutter was set into the cement, and a large manure hatch was on the wall. Along the far end was a milk house with a large pot-belly stove. Nygren opened the hatch beneath the furnace and bent down. He thrust his hand inside and pulled out a large parcel wrapped in cloth.

After lifting the bundle onto the lid of the stove, he opened it. Inside was a green metal box, which was locked, but Nygren opened it with a key. It was full of money. The stacks of bills were wrapped in plastic film and packed as tightly as possible. Raid could see that the bills were all either one-hundred- or two-hundred-euro denominations.

"Rainy day fund. Storms in the forecast."

"And what if someone had lit the stove?" said Raid.

"The flue is closed. It wouldn't have lit and the fabric is fireproof. How much would you guess this is?"

"Hard to say."

"Over half a million."

Nygren's voice was matter of fact. Still, he would

have expected more of a reaction from Raid. Over ten years of hard work, fear and risk, but the spoils measured up.

"I did four years in the clink because of this. Your job is to make sure it wasn't in vain. The money has to go to the right people."

"Right."

Nygren carried the bundle inside and hid it beneath the clothes in his bag.

Raid climbed into the attic to look for the shotgun. An old side-by-side double-barreled Simson was wrapped in construction paper and stashed among some old furniture.

Wrapped up with the weapon was also a box of cartridges. The exterior surface of the barrels was slightly rusty, but oil had protected them on the inside. Raid cocked the shotgun and pulled the trigger twice. The safety didn't work, but otherwise, the weapon was in good shape.

Raid went to the back of the barn to pick a willow switch. He wrapped a piece of fabric around the end and cleaned the oil out of the barrels. Afterwards, he went into the barn and loaded two cartridges. He carried an old metal tub to the end of the barn and fired both barrels one after the other into its side. The cartridges worked flawlessly.

He cleaned the powder and lead residue from the barrels, loaded the gun again and took it with him as he left to warm up the sauna and carry the wash water from the well. Nygren stayed to clean the downstairs of the house.

Raid was an expert at warming saunas. He began with a small flame so the flue, long left unused, could get acclimated. While he waited for that, he sat on the lower bench whittling birch shavings.

Just outside the window, a tall birch was leafing out, and beyond that was the open water of the lake.

Night was beginning to fall.

His father had been fanatical about his saunas, and warming the sauna had always been Raid's job. Sometimes he warmed it five times a week, and always roasting hot. Once, Raid had lost himself in play and it had gotten too late to warm the sauna. He spared himself a beating only by running off into the woods. They searched and called, trying to entice him back, but he lay hidden beneath the low, thick boughs of a spruce, unwilling to budge.

Only after hearing his mother's sobs did he creep carefully toward home. His father had calmed down and his mother was serving fresh pulla rolls with cold milk.

When he aced the sauna heating, his dad rewarded him with a bottle of lemonade.

A shadow flitted past the window and Raid swung the shotgun up in one swift motion. Nygren peeked inside.

"Don't shoot."

He came inside and took a deep breath.

"The smell of smoke on a Saturday night. Only a Finn could know what that means. I'll bet you twenty euros you were thinking the same thing."

"I don't gamble."

Nygren sat down next to him.

"I don't suppose you do much besides work... I didn't have time for much, being in prison and all, but I guess you fared better in that department. You should think about what you'd like to do with your life while you still can. That way you won't have regrets."

Nygren peeked inside the stove and added some wood.

"Strange. When I was your age, I couldn't bear to listen to people's moralizing or the rousing sermons of a bunch of reformed criminals. Now that I think of it, maybe they weren't so fake after all."

Nygren uncapped two bottles of beer and offered one to Raid.

"Maybe most of 'em actually wanted to turn us poor reprobates toward the strait gate and the narrow way."

Nygren straightened up.

"Let's go get something to eat and let the sauna warm up. It's on the house."

Nygren warmed the cabbage rolls in a frying pan and served them up with rye bread and beers. They ate, and by the time they were ready for the sauna, it was nearly dark outside. The electric bulb in the sauna was burnt out, but there was a lantern and some thick candles in the dressing room. Raid brought a candle to the sauna.

Nygren ran a rough sauna. He tossed water on the rocks like a lunatic. Raid wasn't so enthusiastic, but he stayed on the top bench.

"Your father was relentless with the steam," said Nygren. "I'm pretty tough too, but he was more so in that respect. As long as someone else was up there, his *sisu* never let him down… Too bad he was just as stubborn in so many other areas where he should've known enough to give in. He was probably a little too heavy handed with you kids."

"Yeah."

"Your mother was a true gem…in many ways too good for this world, or so it occurred to me on many occasions. There's a lot of your mother in you, at least on the outside. Especially the eyes…"

When they returned to the house it was completely dark out. The light from Raid's lantern lit the path. Nygren tripped over his own feet and fell into some berry bushes. Only after much flailing did he manage to regain his footing.

"Fucking feet are mismatched."

The Cognac was gone and Nygren retrieved another bottle from the car—whiskey this time. He poured half a glass, swirled in some fresh well water and took a seat at the kitchen table. The window looked out onto the road. The nearest neighbor was a couple of hundred yards off. Raid was able to make out the blue glow of a distant television screen from behind the glass.

Nygren slid on his sunglasses and studied the yellow hue of the whiskey against the ceiling light in the kitchen.

"You know why I drink?"

"No."

"Because I'm afraid. Guess what I'm afraid of."

"I'm afraid to guess."

Nygren lowered his voice.

"I'm afraid that someday I'll end up face to face with the people I've wronged. You understand?"

Raid shrugged.

"But it's inevitable. I couldn't die in peace without a reckoning… You'll have your own, sooner or later."

"Right."

"You don't seem to like this subject."

"It's not relevant."

"The sooner you face up to it, the easier for you."

Nygren was so drunk that his head was bobbing.

"I'm gonna make my rounds."

Raid took the shotgun and left.

"You're running from yourself!" Nygren bellowed after him. "You hear me? You're running from yourself!"

Only the light from the kitchen window illuminated the yard. Raid circled the house and stopped every so often to listen.

The branches on the apple tree drummed softly on the metal roof of the house. Raid went to the orchard and lay down on his back in the grass. The tall, dry reeds rustled in the wind on every side. The stars peeked out from behind fast-moving clouds and a half moon hung over the lake, occasionally waning as the clouds scudded past.

A sudden gust of wind shook the apple tree and bent the grass almost to the ground. The bowing blades flicked against Raid's face.

Raid could feel the coolness of the earth through his thin clothing, but he didn't want to get up yet.

He loved wind and storms. When he was a child and a tempest was brewing, he had wrapped himself in a blanket and gone out on the porch. The stronger the storm, the more he enjoyed it. Thunder and lightning only heightened the thrill.

Once, when the forecast had predicted thunderstorms from the south, he had made a pair of wings out of fertilizer sacks and some old lath. He had climbed to the top of a grassy hill that sloped steeply toward a lake and waited there with the wings on his back. When the storm broke, he ran down the hill, leaping as high as he could until the wind filled his wings, threw him to the ground and tore the fabric off the lath.

Another time he had built a tree house high in a dense birch, and when autumn storms arrived, he had crept secretly into the fort to sway in the branches with the wind howling all around.

The moisture in the earth had seeped through his clothes and Raid got up reluctantly.

A moped whined into the neighbor's yard. Its headlight stretched across the field almost to the lake. The driver killed the engine and went inside.

It was quiet again.

Raid went back into the house. The whiskey bottle was on the kitchen table and Nygren lay face down on the living room sofa, breathing heavily. Exhaustion had evidently caught him by surprise.

Raid pulled off Nygren's Mexican boots, lifted his dangling legs back onto the sofa, then tossed a blanket over him.

Afterwards, he locked the door and stacked two pots and a frying pan in front of it.

He took another blanket from the closet, went into the bedroom and turned off the lights. He took off his shoes, but didn't bother with his clothes. Then he watched out the window for a while. The sky was clear, the lake glinting in the moonlight.

Raid lowered himself onto the cot and pulled the covers up to his shoulders.

The television antenna on the roof plinked in the wind like a loose-strung harp. The steel roof rattled.

Raid listened for a moment to the sounds of the night before falling asleep.

# 8.

On Friday, Jansson resolved to put down his own rebellion. If he wasn't going to participate in the rehabilitation, he may as well just leave. But after Anna's visit, he didn't want to anymore.

Jansson resolved to keep his foot on the brake, but still wanted to see what might come of things.

He had been married for thirty years and had never once strayed. On a few occasions, however, he had come close. Most recently a few years prior, when Huusko had coaxed a couple of dozen nursing students into attending the homicide unit's Christmas party. One of the ladies would have readily ravished Jansson if he hadn't fled the scene.

As far as Jansson was concerned, his wife had performed her role so well that he had no reason to complain or prowl.

Up until a few years ago, his wife had been the only woman that he had had sexual dreams about.

Jansson had even bragged to his wife that he was unquestionably the only man in town who had only had sexual dreams about his own wife.

But last night, Jansson had had a sexual dream about Anna. In the dream, Jansson had shed thirty pounds, and his hair was as thick as it was twenty years earlier.

He was on a boat, which he had sold years ago after growing tired of its upkeep. On the boat, he had prepared a glorious dinner, complete with champagne and candles. Anna had stepped in naked. She poured champagne over her head and Jansson had licked it off of her soft skin. The parts he remembered were so prudish that he figured he'd forgotten the more sordid details. They must have been hot, though, as Jansson was full of erotic charge and tender longing when he awoke.

It took a long time before he let go of the dream's satisfying aftermath and fell back asleep.

Before breakfast, Jansson forced himself to consider the situation in the cold light of reason. He knew he was in danger of falling in love. He reminded himself of the unpleasantries that would spawn if he failed to restrain his emotions. In addition to these sensible arguments he cooled himself off by making light of the situation.

In his dream he might be slim, but in reality he was not. In his dream he might be young and virile, but the reality was otherwise. He stood in front of the mirror and forced himself to admit that he couldn't possibly interest a woman of Anna's caliber. With her assets, it would be a simple matter for her to snare one of the local bigwigs.

Jansson swore to himself that, even if for some strange reason Anna had a lust for aging, overweight, balding men with a dry sense of humor, he would not yield to her enticements.

He tracked down his room key and left for breakfast. As he stepped into the hallway, the door to Huusko's room opened and the woman he had been with the previous evening came out putting on an earring. She was wearing the same skirt and scoop-neck blouse as she had the previous evening, and evidently felt guilty, as she startled upon seeing Jansson and hurried downstairs.

Huusko heard Jansson's door shut and peeked into the hallway.

"Boycott's over, huh? Grab a window seat, I'll be right there."

Jansson had wanted to dine in peace and ruminate on his own issues. He knew from experience that Huusko wouldn't give him the opportunity.

Jansson had been advised to eat a light breakfast, but he still hadn't entirely given up on his rebellion. He served himself plenty of ham, cheese and two boiled eggs.

Huusko came to the table and glanced at Jansson's portions.

"Better eat that cholesterol bomb before the guards see you and confiscate it."

Huusko dished himself the same as Jansson and carried it back to the table. He attacked his plate hungrily. Chomping on half an egg, he noted, "I don't have a cholesterol problem. My blood is like a vegan's."

Huusko's bed partner came in, glanced his way, then turned and started to load her tray with food. She had changed into a track suit.

"Whereabouts is she from?" asked Jansson.

"Lappeenranta."

"And what does she do?"

Huusko bit into an open-faced toasted ham sandwich.

"She's a respectable woman... No need to

interrogate her… Works at the Lappeenranta District Customs office."

"You given up on Anna?"

"I've still got a week here. A lot can happen in a week."

Huusko's girl went to a table where three other women were already sitting. The others glanced in Huusko's direction and said something to her. She answered and all four began to laugh.

"Your wife coming on Saturday?"

"She promised to think about it."

"If she doesn't, let's go to town."

"Too old for that."

Huusko glanced back at the group of women, who were still tittering in the corner.

"Women are strange. One night together and they want to wash your clothes and knit you a sweater."

\* \* \*

Jansson had been directed to spend an hour in the gym after breakfast. He shifted from one machine to the next with the trainer at his side.

"Keep it smooth, no jerky movements," the trainer instructed. "Back pain is almost always due to poor muscle tone in your stomach and back. Strong muscles support your spine and keep strains from happening."

Jansson lay on the bench, struggled through five sit-ups and flopped back down, wheezing heavily.

"Take a little breather, then five more."

Jansson rested for a moment before redoubling his efforts. The trainer squatted down at his side.

"One…good. Two…three."

After the third sit-up, Jansson's stomach muscles gave out. The trainer tried to support the small of Jansson's back, but the muscles wouldn't hold.

"I have to say, your abs aren't in very good shape."

"Just a cramp."

The trainer felt Jansson's stomach.

"No cramp, just lack of use."

Huusko came into the gym and proceeded over to where Jansson lay.

"You have some guests in the lobby."

"There are visiting times for guests," said the trainer.

"Official business. Two of Kempas' men— Lunden and Leino. They have some questions about a certain Mister X."

This was Jansson's opportunity.

"Police business."

"This is a physical rehab center, not a police station," the trainer griped.

"When you're indispensable, you're indispensable," said Huusko.

Lunden and Leino were sitting in the lobby. Both were wearing dark suits with ties and had their hair closely cropped. Jansson recalled hearing that Kempas had mandated a suit and tie for everyone on his team.

"Any chance a guy can get some coffee around here?" asked Lunden.

"Yes."

Lunden waited expectantly, but Huusko just sat quietly.

"Huusko," Jansson barked.

Huusko and Lunden got the coffees, and they

settled in at a window table. The veterans' pole-walking club skittered past outside.

"Alright if Huusko sticks around? He was in on the warehouse shooting case."

"Sure," said Leino.

"So what's the problem?"

"We need to figure out what scheme Nygren and this grim reaper Raid are planning. Kempas is convinced they have a major gig in the works. They were last seen in Kuopio the day before last. Apparently, a couple of Nygren's former accomplices want a cut of his money. They had a little skirmish at a gas station."

"Who won?" asked Huusko.

"Nygren and Raid, five-zip."

Jansson sipped his coffee.

"What do you need me for?"

"You know Raid better than anybody else. Kempas mentioned that he talked about it on the phone with you, but he thought it best if we met face to face. This joint just happened to be on the way."

"So Kempas thinks I'm hiding something from him?"

Lunden interjected.

"Here's the thing. Unless we figure out what they're up to, we'll be Kempas' lackeys for life. You know how he is. No going home until the job is done. We'd be much obliged for any crumbs you can spare."

Lunden's sincerity worked with Jansson.

"Raid called me."

"He called? What'd he say?"

"He knows the cops are after them. Said they have no criminal intentions."

"You believe him?"

Jansson nodded.

Leino glanced at Lunden before speaking. "We've learned that Nygren is terminally ill."

"That I didn't know."

"According to our sources he has cancer. In that case, the only gig he's planning is a funeral."

"So Kempas thinks Nygren is faking it?"

"He's convinced that Nygren's so crooked he'd believe anything about the guy. But if Nygren is dying, then why's he traipsing around the country?"

"Maybe he wants to visit some places that are important to him before he dies. A kind of pilgrimage."

"Sounds plausible, but what's Raid doing with him?"

"Anyone who's terminally ill probably needs a little help."

"Is that what he said, or are you inferring that?"

"I'm inferring."

"Did he say anything else?"

"Nothing that would have any significance."

"Do you have the number to his cellphone?"

"No."

"Did he say where he was calling from?"

"Listen, am I a cop or a mini-mart cashier?"

"Sorry."

"We'd be much obliged if you'd let us know if he calls again. Once we get on their trail, we'll try to stay on it."

"I know Kempas is a capable cop, but I don't see any benefit in having Nygren and Raid followed, especially when they know the cops are after them."

"To be frank, neither do we, but I know how his

brain works. His theory is the more you look around, the more you see and hear. In the field, you might get a lead. At your desk, you just get hemorrhoids."

"Lots of wisdom in that," Jansson allowed.

They watched as Lunden and Leino walked across the parking lot to their car. The men looked more like salesmen than policemen.

"You think I should make suits mandatory for the department?"

"And miniskirts for the ladies," said Huusko. "Then again, Susisaari's the only one on the force with legs. Everyone else has stumps."

"Not nice, Huusko."

"But true."

* * *

After lunch, Jansson was resting in his room when the telephone rang. It was Anna.

"I hear you're showing your face in public again."

"I had to. My fans demanded it."

"I want to chat about something with you...I need some advice."

"What about?"

"Is it alright if we meet this evening?"

"Where?"

"How about in front of the main entrance at seven? You can get in your evening walk at the same time."

"See you there."

Jansson put down the phone and it promptly rang again. This time it was his wife.

"The line was busy. Who were you talking to?"

"Work."

"Poor dear…they still won't leave you alone?"

"What do you want?"

"What do I want? Can't I just call?"

"Of course."

"Don't snap at me just because you're having a hard time. Try taking it like a grown man."

"Are you coming on Saturday?"

"If you act like that, definitely not."

"I promise to be good."

"Have you lost weight?"

"A few pounds."

"At least it's something."

"Forty pounds would be something."

"I like to have something to hold onto."

"I gotta go."

"Why?"

"There's a dance starting downstairs."

"That's the kind of hanky-panky they encourage there? Remember to keep your paws off those sixty-year-old bimbos."

"There're younger ladies here too."

"That goes for them too, then. You can look, but don't touch."

"You coming on Saturday?"

"Oh, alright."

* * *

Jansson felt as if he were thirty years younger. He was getting ready to meet a woman who had played the leading role in the previous night's erotic dream.

Jansson stepped into the shower, washed what little hair he had and combed it in front of the mirror until he was satisfied. Afterwards, he trimmed his overgrown eyebrows and the hairs jutting out of his ears with the scissors on his Swiss army knife.

His wife, perceptive as she was, had always maintained that beneath his façade of modesty, Jansson was an exceptionally vain man. He double checked to be sure that no nose hairs were visible and slathered his chin liberally with aftershave.

He slipped on some casual slacks, a thick blue sweater and a sporty-looking windbreaker.

Jansson was waiting in front of the door at seven minutes till seven. The dance was just starting, and people were milling about in the lobby. Jansson edged a bit further away from the door and waited under a maple that was growing in front of the building. He didn't want there to be any witnesses to their meeting.

Anna came around the corner at two minutes till. She had on jeans and a thick pea coat.

She slipped her arm casually under Jansson's and pulled him along.

"Beautiful weather. Feels like August."

Jansson was quiet. Though he enjoyed her touch, he felt tense.

"What was your question?"

"Once a cop, always a cop. Straight to the point."

"Does it concern Huusko?"

"No…it's about my ex-husband."

The road to town was lit, but beyond that were fields and forests. About a quarter of a mile away, the lights of the nearest farm were visible. The sky was bristling with stars.

"What about him?"

"I've been wondering how to put this without you misunderstanding."

"Just tell it like it is."

"We would have divorced even if he never found out about Huusko. I would've never gone so far with Huusko if my marriage hadn't already been over."

The lights of a passenger plane approached from the north, swept overhead and continued southward. Anna stopped.

"Wish I was headed south on that plane, away from all this lifeless gloom."

"What about your husband?"

"He's threatening me... I don't know what to do..."

"What do you mean by 'threatening?' Has he threatened to hurt you? Or something else?"

"He said I'm in trouble if I don't agree to his demands."

"And what are those?"

"When we divorced he was quite well-to-do... The flat in Helsinki went to me, and I've been renting it out ever since I moved here. Now he's in financial trouble and wants me to sell the apartment and split the money."

"If he's threatened you, you can press charges against him."

Anna took Jansson's hand and pressed it between hers.

"Must everything be so formal... Couldn't we take care of it...kinda off the record..."

"What do you mean?"

"If for example a detective lieutenant called him... I think it might scare him..."

"You mean me?"

"Yes."

Jansson's expression turned dour.

"I don't think that's going to work."

"Of course, you'd be compensated for your trouble... I plan to sell the flat and can make a pretty nice profit on it right now..."

Jansson's expression went from dour to surly. In one fell swoop, the romantic surge he had felt in his chest faded away. Anna's lips were set in a smile full of promise, but her charm no longer worked.

Jansson pried his hand away from hers and said with unnecessary gruffness, "You can't buy a policeman, at least not me."

Anna realized she had made a mistake.

"I'm sorry... I'm just afraid of him... I only meant to ask for advice. From an experienced officer."

"My advice is that you contact the local police department directly."

Inside, the first waltz of the evening began to drift outside.

"How about if we go inside," said Jansson.

Anna didn't reply, but followed him nonetheless.

# 9.

Raid awoke at seven in the morning and checked the vicinity of the house. Afterwards, he went to the sauna to wash up. There was still a trace of warmth in the stove's water basin. After breakfast, he inspected the car: checked the oil and radiator fluid, kicked the tires and carried the bulk of their luggage into the car. Nygren's shotgun was within reach the entire time.

The neighbors were up as well. The farmer was towing hay bales out of the fields into the barn. Winter was coming, and much faster than city people realized. The bustling put-put of the tractor was the only sound around.

Raid had spent his childhood in the country and knew the rituals of rural life, the intimate connection people had with the seasons, the weather and work. Every season had its own chores, to be done promptly. Nature rarely forgave delays—frost set in, snow fell, rains flooded and drought gave rise to fires. There was always something to fear. In light of all the dangers that stalked farmers, Raid considered it a miracle that the country could feed itself.

The neighboring farmer didn't intend to let the hay go late. He dumped a load of hay into the barn and set off immediately for another load. The rear-end of the trailer tossed wildly on the bumpy road. Then the tractor suddenly swerved like a race car and made off across the field.

Nygren woke up around ten, looking grizzled and out of sorts. Raid had cleared the kitchen table and set out breakfast for him: juice, yogurt, eggs, bread and coffee.

"Alright if I pay for my stupidity in silence?" asked Nygren.

"Sure."

Nygren wet his head with water from the wash bucket and dried his hair on a towel. Then he grabbed the glass of juice, gulped it down, and filled it up again.

"I suppose I said some things."

"Right."

"My intentions were good, but maybe the goal was a little unclear. Did I quote the Bible?"

"That too."

"I used to read it every day in prison. It can stick with you... Besides, it's a very wise book."

Raid took the coffee off the stove and poured some for Nygren.

The sky was partly cloudy and the wind was brisk. From the window, whitecaps were visible on the lake. The neighbor's twenty-odd cows were ranging across the field toward the shore. This was one of their last opportunities to enjoy the open air. Soon, they'd be locked in the barn and strapped to a milking machine for the winter. Poor producers would be weeded out and given an ample dose of voltage for their final meal.

Nygren shook his head between his hands.

"This is what I'd call a hangover... It's hard to be

a hospitable neighbor—these country bumpkins are so fond of their liquor."

Nygren went to the kitchen cabinet and took a box of aspirin off the shelf. He gulped down two tablets and a chaser of well water.

"Eat something, it should help," said Raid.

Nygren looked at Raid and smiled.

"Easy boy… This isn't the first hangover of my life…though it might be the last."

The neighbor throttled the tractor back toward home again. He didn't seem bothered by any hangover. Nygren watched him go.

"A nice guy otherwise, but likes his liquor."

This time the tractor didn't turn toward the barn, but continued on toward Nygren's house.

Nygren followed the approaching tractor over the rim of his coffee cup.

"What'd I tell you. He's coming to see if there's anything left over."

Nygren didn't have the strength to get up and greet him, so he sat and waited. Still loaded with a few bales of hay, the tractor stopped in the middle of the yard. The neighbor didn't get out, just sat fidgeting with something on the dashboard.

Raid noticed the neighbor's averted gaze and climbed upstairs with the shotgun. Carefully, he peeked outside. From above, he could see the bed of the trailer spread out like a banquet.

Raid went back downstairs. Nygren was gathering what strength he had to greet the visitor.

"Tell him to come inside," said Raid.

Nygren gave him a look, but did as he was told. He cracked the door just enough to squeeze his head out.

"Care for some coffee, neighbor?"

The farmer pushed the sliding window aside.

"You wouldn't happen to have a screwdriver? Something's wrong with the ignition."

"I doubt it."

"Even a butter knife would do. Or a little coin…just something to turn this."

Raid handed Nygren a knife.

"Give it to him from the right side of the tractor."

Nygren looked wonderingly at Raid, but pulled on his boots and stepped outside. Raid circled around to the back yard via the cellar door. By circling the house, he was able to get within about thirty feet of the trailer's left side. Nygren stood next to the tractor, chatting with the neighbor.

"This has never… Something goofy with this…"

Raid made a swift dive toward the side of the trailer and came up next to it. He saw that the neighbor had noticed him.

"You takin' off today already?" the neighbor asked, winking at Nygren.

"As soon as this hangover lets up…"

Nygren peered about.

"Could've used the company. Done some fishing or hunting… The rabbits are overrunning the place…"

Raid circled to the rear of the trailer and carefully opened one of the hooks on the tailgate. Once he opened the other, the tailgate slammed down and Raid could see directly into the bed. Sariola was just behind the tractor with a pistol, his stocky body huddled up on all fours. Lehto lay along the edge of the trailer holding a baseball bat.

Sariola wheeled and fired at Raid, who managed

to shove a hay bale into the line of fire. The bullet struck the bale and buried itself inside.

Raid stepped aside and saw Nygren and the neighbor diving for cover behind the tractor. Sariola was set to fire again and Raid didn't wait any longer. He fired one of the barrels from a low angle. Sariola's gun and a couple of fingers splattered against the back window of the tractor.

Raid fell back far enough that he could see Sariola over the edge of the bed. Sariola was staggering to his feet while holding his right hand with his left. Blood gushed out from between his fingers and streamed down his sleeve.

"The bat!" Raid shouted. "Throw it on the ground!"

Lehto's bat promptly flew over the edge of the bed.

"Any more weapons?"

"No."

"Get out!"

Lehto wasted no time. Sariola didn't seem to have heard the command. He just swayed on the trailer bed, fighting to stay conscious. Seeing his own blood was the worst thing he knew.

"He lost some fingers," Lehto reported.

Nygren picked up Lehto's baseball bat, and he and the neighbor came to Raid's aid.

"Everything alright?"

"Yeah."

"I thought he got you."

"He got the hay bale."

Raid swung himself onto the trailer with his gun at the ready. Sariola had fallen onto a hay bale.

The neighbor glanced into the trailer with an

apologetic expression.

"They threatened me with a gun...caught me off guard as I was coming in from the fields. I tried to wink, but my face felt kinda stiff..."

They brought Sariola down and carried him into the kitchen of the house. Nygren got some bandages and wrapped the torn-up hand as best he could. The index and middle fingers of the right hand were severed at the middle joint, and the other fingers were riddled with buckshot. Some of the shot had gotten past his hand and hit him in the shoulder.

"The vein is severed. He needs a hospital or he'll bleed to death," said Nygren.

"Where'd you leave the car," Raid asked Lehto.

"At the edge of the woods."

"I'd suggest you drive him to the hospital. The other option is worse for all of us, especially you two."

"Alright...alright."

Raid slapped him across the face.

"Got that?"

"Yes, I got it. Trust me, I've had enough. Doesn't matter if you got a hundred mil... I swear..."

They lifted the fading Sariola onto the trailer bed and drove him and Lehto to their car. Lehto laid some coats on the back seat and they lifted him inside.

Raid guided Lehto into the car.

"On the way there you can think of some explanation that doesn't involve us."

The neighbor offered a suggestion.

"Hunting accident. Dog knocked over the shotgun and it went off. It's happened before."

Lehto nodded and drove off.

Raid and Nygren rode back to the house in the

trailer. There, the neighbor hopped out of the cab and walked up to them. He had been thinking about the incident.

"I ain't got nothin' against you, and don't need to know about it. If anyone asks, I didn't see anything, and I'll clean the blood off the tractor."

Nygren put his hand on the man's shoulder.

"Thank you. You're a good neighbor."

The neighbor looked at Raid reverently.

"Gotta admit you took care of those goons pretty nicely... Doesn't even work that slick in the pictures."

"Thanks."

Raid went to clean the blood stains off the kitchen floor. Nygren opened a beer and sat down to watch.

"Think they've had enough?"

"Hopefully."

"Does it bother you that I'm drinking? Got a nice bender going."

"No."

Raid tossed the bloody rag into the wood stove, where the embers from the morning's coffee were still glowing. The rag burst slowly into flames.

"Not much seems to bother you... You blow a guy's fingers to smithereens, clean up the mess like you were doing dishes, and then you're done."

"Right."

# 10.

Detective Lieutenant Kempas was flying to Kuopio. Not by helicopter—by an ordinary passenger plane. Leino and Lunden were waiting in the airport cafeteria, and they watched as Kempas exited the plane under the curious gaze of the flight attendant.

"He's been digging through the family wardrobe again."

Kempas was wearing a narrow-brimmed hat straight out of the 1960s, a long, dark-grey coat, white shirt, and narrow-cut necktie. With his slim suitcase, he looked like a gangster out of a 1960s British thriller.

In a weak moment, Kempas had revealed that he had inherited his uncle's estate: about ten nearly unused suits and other clothes. Once they had fallen out of fashion, his wealthy uncle had abandoned the suits to a wardrobe, but Kempas was no slave to fashion.

"Should we stop at the hotel before going to the hospital?" asked Leino.

"The hospital first."

Lunden took the wheel and Leino slid in beside him. Kempas took the back seat for himself.

"How's Sariola doing?"

"He had surgery on his hand. Just flesh wounds in the shoulder. Nothing serious."

"Is he talking?"

"He claims he doesn't know who shot him, nor is he accusing anyone."

"What about Nygren and his friend?"

"We're searching 'round the clock, but nothing. If Nygren has a phone, it's not in his name."

Kempas wrinkled his brow irritably.

"Nice going. The crooks are having a laugh."

"According to Jansson, this Raid called him from a prepaid cell phone and the caller ID was blocked. I think he's telling the truth."

"He's hiding something. Not sure what, but I can smell it."

"How long's this gonna take?" Leino ventured to ask. "I only ask because the wife is turning forty in three days."

"As long as it takes."

As Kempas was not in a chatty mood, Lunden and Leino thought it wisest to remain silent. Kempas took a notepad from his pocket and began jotting notes with a look of consternation on his face. Every so often, he underlined a few words with bold strokes.

"Is Sariola under protection?" said Kempas without raising his eyes from the notepad.

"No. We don't have the authorization or grounds for that. He should be safe here in the hospital."

"Either one of you could've stayed to stand guard. I only need one driver."

In a bad mood, Kempas was like a wife who knew her husband's every weakness, knew how to hit him where it hurt the most.

"What about this other guy, Lehto?"

"We have an APB out on him."

"An actual APB... It'd be nice if he were actually found."

Irritated by Kempas' comment, Lunden let out the clutch too fast and he ground the gears.

"Is that the car's fault or the driver's?" Kempas scoffed.

Lunden recalled a particularly harsh teacher from his grade school years. The cranky old man had employed a similar tone of voice, but had bolstered his message by twisting students' ears or yanking the hair at the napes of their necks. Lunden swept his hand instinctively across his ear. He remembered all too well how the bullying felt.

"One thing's for sure, the car's a piece of shit," he said.

"I doubt you'd make the police racing team either."

"I would if I could get some decent sponsors."

Kempas' expression softened. Lunden caught it in the rear-view mirror and commended himself for the quip.

* * *

Sariola had been furnished with a private room. He lay on the bed with his upper body in bandages. The thigh on his right leg was also bandaged. On the nightstand was a pitcher of juice, a mug, a banana and a package of salmiakki salt licorice. Kempas took a chair and seated himself next to the bed. Lunden and Leino remained standing.

"Sorry we didn't bring flowers. How are you feeling?" Kempas began.

"Like shit."

"A familiar feeling. I'm Detective Lieutenant Kempas from the Helsinki police. I'm not interested in you or even this shooting. I'm looking for Nygren."

"Good."

"With your help, I can put him in some deep shit."

"Even better."

"What's Nygren planning?"

"How the fuck should I know?"

"You've been on a few jobs with him. You know him pretty well."

"I ain't no mindreader. Not that it would hold up in court anyway."

"Who shot you?"

"I wish I knew."

"I gotta say, I'd think you'd be able to hold your own against an old guy like Nygren. He's almost sixty... And to think someone claimed you're a pretty tough customer."

"Think whatever you want."

"And there were two of you guys, too. Pretty sad."

Leino had to admit, the scorn in Kempas' voice was every bit as difficult to resist as scratching a juicy itch.

"We arrested Lehto," Kempas lied. "You wanna see him?"

"What the hell for!"

"I figured you're friends since you're always together. Lehto's a softy; he's worried about you."

Sariola didn't respond.

"Do you know who Nygren's friend was? The one who poured hot coffee on your nuts?"

Sariola's eyes blazed, but he didn't respond.

"We do. You wanna know?"

Sariola nodded.

"Not sure if I should bother telling you. The guy actually did a good deed."

"Eat shit."

"How are your balls doing, by the way? Itchy? Why aren't you scratching?"

Brazenly, Kempas helped himself to a handful of Sariola's candy.

"Who is he?" Sariola bleated.

"You sure fucked up. He's the wrong guy to play hardball with."

"Who is he?"

"I hear you and Nygren argued about money. Did he scam you?"

"Tell me who that guy is, first."

"You really wanna know?" Kempas jiggled his carrot.

"Tell me."

"He kills bugs dead."

"Raid! That guy was Raid? *The* Raid?"

"You oughta thank God you're still alive. After a run-in with Raid, not many are."

"Nygren claimed the guy was his nephew."

Kempas let out a series of cackles.

"Nephew. And you swallowed it hook, line and sinker. Nygren's a pretty sharp guy for a crook. While you both served time, the money earned interest in Nygren's account."

Sariola clenched his one good hand into a fist.

"Care for some coffee?"

"No."

"Smoke?"

"No."

"Candy?"

Kempas shook the package.

"It's empty."

Kempas glanced at Leino.

"When's Lehto gonna be here?"

Leino glanced over at Lunden.

"I'll go call."

"You do that. If he behaves, he can see his friend."

"I don't wanna see that chickenshit."

"How come?"

"It's enough that I say no. This ain't no prison, it's a hospital. And I'm not a suspect. Or am I?"

"Not for anything other than stupidity. Help us get Nygren and you can get even."

"How?"

"We'll throw him in the clink."

"Why? What'd he do?"

"That's what I'm asking you. Give us a reason to lock him up. We could easily get him for attempted murder. Same goes for Raid."

"I don't know anything about his plans. He's probably planning something, considering he's got that thug with him."

"What'd he say to you at the bar?"

"What do you mean?"

"What was that fight about?"

"I asked for a loan."

"And Nygren wouldn't help out an old friend?"

"Listen, I've been shot in two places. I could use some rest."

"Where's Nygren now?" Kempas persisted.

"No idea."

"Where were you when Raid shot you?"

Sariola fell silent again.

"Alright…then we'll find out when we talk with Lehto. I could've put a little gold star on your chart, you know. Stars are worth their weight in gold if you happen to need the cops' help…mine for instance. Stars can get you a shorter sentence and other perks. But if you can't appreciate it, I'll give it to Lehto. I'm sure he collects stars."

"Who told you Raid shot me?"

"I don't need to tell you that."

"Well, I might be able to tell you where they're shacked up."

Kempas glanced at Leino.

"Kari, grab us some coffee and pastries."

Kempas turned to Sariola.

"Cream or black?"

"Cream and three sugar cubes."

"Cream and three sugar cubes," Kempas repeated. "And bring us a good map while you're at it."

* * *

Kempas, Leino and Lunden were at Nygren's farm in just over an hour. They left the car behind a ridge and studied the house through binoculars.

"No sign of life and no car, unless it's in the barn."

They waited about fifteen minutes, but when nothing happened, Kempas went up to the house with his hand on the butt of his gun. He was needlessly cautious—the place was empty. He brashly busted the glass on the porch door and opened it.

It was evident the house had been occupied recently. The downstairs had been cleaned and the new dust hadn't had time to settle yet.

Kempas took a look in the refrigerator. Inside were a few beers, a bottle of mustard and a stick of butter. A tabloid newspaper lay on the living room table. It was a couple of days old.

"We just missed them," said Lunden.

Kempas went upstairs, searched every closet and glanced up into the attic.

He then went back outside and headed for the barn.

He didn't need to break into the barn. The door was latched but not locked. Kempas climbed into the loft and kicked some hay around. He found a *Cocktail* men's magazine from the 1960s that had been stashed in a hole in the wall. Kempas riffled through a few wrinkled pages. The naked women looked like German lot lizards. He tossed the magazine into the corner.

Next, Kempas stepped into the sauna building. Some soap had dried on the dressing room bench, and beneath it were three beer bottles.

"The neighbor might know when they left," Lunden said. "The road goes right past the house."

The nearest house was a few hundred yards away. In the yard was an orange Russian-made Lada from the 1980s, popular cars with Finnish farmers because of their low cost. A black moped stood nearby. A Spitz on a tie-out bounded up to them barking, and somebody parted the curtains.

Kempas knocked on the door a few times, then stepped inside. The house's owner was already on his way to the door.

"Hello," said Kempas.

The man nodded. He had apparently been napping, as he looked drowsy.

"Police. I'm Detective Lieutenant Kempas. I'm interested in your neighbor, but he's already gone. Do you know when he left?"

The neighbor scratched his stubbly chin.

"What neighbor you talkin' about?"

Kempas sensed the man's stalling tactics, but didn't let that discourage him.

"Up on the hill by the lake."

"Oh, that one?"

"Yes, that one."

"They were still around yesterday."

"What about today?"

"Haven't seen 'em today."

"Have you been here all day?"

"Wouldn't say that. I been cuttin' down trees in the woods out past the lower forty since seven in the morning. Can't see here from there."

"When's the last time you saw them yesterday?"

"Sometime in the evening, I think."

"And who'd you see?"

"The owner, this Nygren. The other I didn't recognize."

"Did anyone else come to the house?"

"If they did, I didn't see 'em."

"Did you hear anything out of the ordinary, gunshots or anything like that?"

"Absolutely not."

The statement was emphatic enough that Kempas knew the man was lying.

"Absolutely not. Pretty strong words," said Kempas.

"Does Nygren own the property?" asked Leino.

"That's my understanding, unless he sold it."

"How long has he owned it?"

"Oh, about five years now."

"Does he come here often?"

"Probably been a year since he was here last...
What are you fellas chasin' him for, a nice guy like
him?"

Kempas looked the neighbor straight in the eyes.

"You'll swear under oath you don't know
anything more?"

"I've had a reputation as an honest man my whole
life."

"Then you have nothing to be afraid of. What kind
of car were they driving?"

"Nygren's old Benz."

"You swore under oath you were disclosing
everything. Why'd you leave out the Mercedes?"

"What oath was that again?" the neighbor asked
hesitantly.

"You have anything else?"

"No, but what oath..."

"The oath of an honest Finn."

Kempas left his words hanging in the air as he
departed.

In the yard, the dog came charging up again.
Lunden picked up a stick and threw it behind the
doghouse. The dog didn't give it so much as a glance.

"You can't trust these hicks."

* * *

Back at the hotel, Kempas couldn't bring himself to
take a break and unpack his meager luggage. Instead,
he picked up his notepad and commenced with
dispensing orders.

"Kari, you find out from the Land Registry who

really owns Nygren's place. Seppo, organize a proper search of the place: men, a dog and a mine sweeper. It's likely Sariola was shot there. I'll go have a chat with Nygren's daughter... If Nygren's been around these parts, he's probably gone to see her."

"How are we supposed to justify the search with the local PD?" asked Lunden.

"Attempted murder, potential drug-related crimes. The house could be a base for stolen goods...or a moonshine factory. Anything."

Lunden took his leave, but stopped in the doorway.

"Just one question. Do you have something personal against Nygren?"

Kempas stared cuttingly at Lunden.

"Yes."

"Can I ask why?"

"Sure, but you won't get an answer."

# 11.

A little boy of about six was swinging wildly on the swingset. With every flick of his legs he gained speed, and his rubber boots cleared the cross bar every time. On his head was a red cap and he wore a thick pair of overalls.

The swing was located in the yard of a 1970s apartment building. The area was rife with many more of the same grey pre-fab buildings, separated by sparse clumps of pines. Each building had its own parking lot filled with lower-middle-class vehicles. Next to each lot stood a garbage shed. The play area, with its swings and sandboxes, was shared by three buildings.

Nygren had cranked the car window down halfway and was watching the boy.

"Lively little fella."

"He likes speed."

Nygren held a photograph in his hand. In the picture, the boy on the swing sat in the lap of a woman in her thirties. The picture had been taken at Tampere's Särkänniemi amusement park with various rides and the Näsinneula observation tower in the background. The boy was wearing the same red cap he had on now. The woman had wrapped her arm around the boy as if afraid of losing him in the bustle of the amusement park.

The boy slowed up some and leaped off the swing into a sand pile he had heaped up in front of the sandbox.

Nygren put the photo back in his wallet and took out a second. This one was a faded old color photograph. The picture showed a seven- or eight-year-old girl with a black-and-white kitten in her lap.

"I gave her that kitten for her seventh birthday. Its name was Miumau. Jaana's cousins drowned it in a pond. Tied a rock around its neck and tossed it in. Jaana sent me a letter about it and asked me to come give them all a thrashing."

"Did you?"

"Wanted to. I would've bought her another kitten, but she didn't want one."

"When's the last time you saw her?"

"At her confirmation. Over fifteen years ago."

Nygren got out of the car; Raid did not. Nygren turned and gestured for him to follow.

"You don't need me."

"I'm too nervous to go alone. To just show up out of nowhere after so long."

Raid stepped out of the car, but lagged back.

The boy was building his sand pile up even bigger with a plastic shovel. He was so lost in his work that he didn't even notice the visitors.

"Hi," said Nygren.

The boy turned to look, lifted the brim of his cap and squinted his eyes.

"Hi."

"I saw you swinging. Don't think I've ever seen anyone swing so high."

"Mika's even better," said the boy, though he was clearly delighted by the praise.

"Is your mom home?"

"Yeah. I'm goin' to eat pretty soon. We're having macaroni casserole."

"Probably your favorite, huh?"

"Yeah."

The boy kicked shyly at the sand pile.

"Who're you?"

"Jari!"

The shout came from the nearest building, where a woman in a wool sweater and skirt was standing under the porch watching. Then she approached them. It was the same woman from the amusement park photo. She came to the boy's side and stared at Nygren, who smiled stiffly.

"Hi Jaana."

She pulled the boy close, as if shielding him from danger.

"What do you want?"

She tried to keep her composure, but her voice was wavering.

"Who's that man?"

"Your grandfather."

"Grandpa?"

"You know me after all," Nygren smiled.

Nygren and Jaana looked at one another.

"I was just on my way north and thought I'd visit."

Nygren nodded toward Raid.

"The both of us."

The woman glanced at Raid before turning back to Nygren.

"We'll be on our way... I just wanted to see you.

Nothing more... And the boy, of course. Just as lively as you were at that age."

The woman was toying with a gold pendant around her neck, a small angel with outspread wings.

"You still have that."

"It's been almost twenty years since... You haven't visited, haven't sent a card, you don't call... Then suddenly you show up when your grandson is six..."

"I didn't want to interfere with your lives. I've been asking Eila about you and she's sent some pictures... You probably won't believe me, but I've prayed for you many nights."

"What, in prison?"

"Well...there too."

"Grandpa was in prison?" the boy asked.

"You'd better go."

Nygren slipped a thick envelope and a folded sheet of paper out of his coat pocket. He unfolded the paper.

"I found this when I was going through my things... I wrote it to you when you were one."

Nygren stared at the letter, gathering his courage.

"My dear Jaana, sleep beckons till tomorrow. I hope that night and day will leave you free of sorrow..."

He swallowed and cleared his throat.

"With light, my dear, you'll play outdoors. You've boundless love; the world's a friend of yours..."

His voice dwindled to a whisper.

"The grass, my dear, will whisper words of gladness. Laugh, enjoy the day, and turn away from sadness."

Nygren folded the paper and handed it and the envelope to Jaana.

"I'd like to give this to you. Open it inside."

Nygren pressed the envelope into her hand. She hesitated briefly before taking it. Nygren raised his hand to her face and lightly stroked her cheek.

"Farewell."

The woman hung her head.

"I want grandpa to come inside. I wanna show him my new car."

Nygren squatted down next to the boy and grasped his hand.

"Some other time. Grandpa's going to Lapland for a fall hike. Where Santa lives. I'll tell him you're a good boy and he'll bring you lots of presents."

"I'd like more Legos."

"I'll tell him, but you have to be a good boy and do as your mom says."

Nygren's voice cracked and he straightened up and turned to walk toward the car. Now, like most others his age, he suddenly seemed to stoop as he walked.

Raid gave Jaana a nod before following Nygren.

* * *

Raid and Nygren had dinner at the hotel restaurant. Nygren ordered a bottle of red wine and drank all but a glass of it. He took a Cognac with his coffee.

It was just past seven o'clock and the hotel band was tuning up in the adjacent room. Nygren was clearly irritated by the noise. He sipped his drink at a feverish pace and shifted restlessly in his chair. Raid could see that he couldn't get the meeting with his daughter out of his mind. He was drinking to forget.

"How much do I have to pay you to shoot them all? The whole band."

"You'd get a volume discount."

Nygren took a nip of Cognac and stared at Raid.

"Just a few days left. You sure you're with me?"

"In this profession you ruin your reputation if you break a promise."

"Does that mean something to you?"

"Everything."

"That's how I used to think. Then I realized that a reputation is like a woman. If you act too interested, she vanishes. But if you're indifferent, she hangs on your coattails, begging for attention. Once I stopped giving a shit, I started having to shovel reputation off my back. It was coming in from everywhere. I'm talking about the reputation you get in this line of work."

"I'll keep that in mind."

"I'm serious."

"So am I."

"You're father was very talkative, and your mother had quite the lively tongue too. How the hell did you turn out so tight-lipped?"

"I'm a good listener."

"That you are, I must admit... What'd you think of my daughter...and her boy?"

"You have good reason to be proud of both."

"The meeting was a little clumsy...but I suppose anybody would be a little surprised if the old man suddenly popped up after being gone for twenty years."

"True."

"If I'd let her know in advance, she...she might

not have come, though I'd have understood. In the end, I made the choice, not her, and not her mother."

The band's drummer banged out a blinding drum solo that threatened to break the sound barrier.

"Starting to fucking piss me off…"

Nygren's speech broke off abruptly and he clutched at his stomach. His face knotted up in a painful grimace. He tried to stand, but toppled backward, knocking over a neighboring table that had just been set. His breath came in broken gasps, and a continuous wheezing sounded from his lips.

Raid grabbed the nearest waitress.

"An ambulance! Quick!"

He pushed her on her way and bent down next to Nygren.

"My stomach… Hurts like hell…"

Nygren's words dissolved into a groan.

Raid snatched a pillow off a sofa next to the wall and slipped it under Nygren's head. Nygren was trembling uncontrollably, but he kept trying to heave himself up.

"Just stay down," Raid commanded as he pressed him back into a lying position.

He held Nygren down for almost ten minutes before the medics dashed in with a stretcher.

One of them bent down to examine Nygren.

"What's wrong?"

"Severe stomach pain," Raid replied.

They hoisted Nygren onto the stretcher. Raid followed close behind. The waitress stopped him at the exit.

"Who's going to pay the bill? It came to almost a hundred."

Raid took a few bills out of his pocket and tossed them over his shoulder.

* * *

The hospital cafeteria was a dreary place. Raid sat next to the window, drinking his second cup of coffee. Seated near him were two patients dressed in hospital gowns. A young woman behind the counter was lining up packages of cookies. She looked at Raid and pointed to a clock on the wall. A couple minutes till nine.

"We're closing soon," she said, just to be sure. "You want anything else?"

Raid bought a chocolate bar and an orange juice and went into the waiting room where about ten people sat. A black woman had two children—an infant in her lap and a boy of about three or four running up and down the hallway. At least the runner didn't seem to be in need of any medical attention.

An older woman waited across the room, her body wrapped in a peculiar-looking fabric, a huge knit hat covering her hair. In her lap, she held a faux-leather tote bag. Every now and then she muttered something, but so quietly that Raid couldn't catch it.

There were also two young men in the room, one of whom had a bruised and bloodied face. The other was apparently just his companion. A drunk with bronzed skin sat apart from the others wearing a thick, gray ulster and a ratty hat. He had something against the youngsters.

"Ought to strangle those kinda punks in the cradle...not let 'em grow up and start trouble..."

"Go hang yourself, gramps."

An ambulance pulled up to the main entrance with its sirens blaring, and two nurses ran out to meet it. A bloodied man emerged on a stretcher. Though the crown of his skull was hemorrhaging blood, he was conscious and shouting in a loud voice.

"Gimme back my damn shotgun and I'll end this right now. I ain't gonna sponge off these right-wing assholes. Better off dead than unemployed."

The man was fighting so hard to right himself that blood and some peculiar sludge spurted out of his wound and splattered at the youngsters' feet. The beaten guy's friend bent down to have a closer look.

"Fuck! That's a blob of brain there."

"Yeah, right," said the other.

"Look!"

"Fuck, it's just goop or snot, or something."

"Didn't you see he had half his head missing? He was yelling for his shotgun—probably shot himself in the head. That's brains, man, how much you wanna bet."

The man's shouts grew fainter as the entourage retreated down the hallway.

Raid walked to the window. Outside, it was raining. The hospital was high on a hill with the town spread out below. Just in front of the hospital was a grassy field, and beyond that a fire station and an auto repair shop. From there, apartment buildings sprawled into the distance. A few scattered cars scudded along the rain-soaked streets.

"What the fuck...that dude is shitting his pants. Shit is dropping out of his pants onto the floor!"

The kid hopped up and marched over to the receptionist's desk.

"That wino shit his pants. How's anyone supposed

to sit here with that awful smell?"

The receptionist peeked out from behind the glass.

"We don't have custodians on duty at this hour."

"I sure ain't gonna clean it up. You work here—do something about it. I can't breathe in here."

The stench began to spread throughout the room. The black woman gathered her children and moved off to the hallway about fifty feet away. The boys went into the entryway.

Only the perpetrator was unfazed by the uproar. He wagged his trouser leg and the last of his load tumbled onto the floor. The incident inspired a pensive, somewhat melancholy statement from him.

"In the end, we all turn to shit. Only the soul has to be cared for…has to be kept clean."

The receptionist finally saw fit to intervene. She came out from behind the counter and looked at the mess.

"The restroom is just across the room. Did he have to do it here?"

"Yes, actually, in that very spot. That there's the protest of a private citizen and former taxpayer. You've held me up here for half a day, with no end in sight. Mocking a man who served in the war…"

The drunk's eyes clouded over and tears welled up in his eyes.

"Not even treated like a human anymore…"

Just then, a stout man in a white coat strode briskly into the room. There was no mistaking his profession. In his breast pocket was a plastic badge with the name Dr. Rimpinen.

"Who here is with Nygren?"

"I am," said Raid.

The man sniffed the air and whisked Raid into the

adjoining room.

"Are you a relative?"

Raid nodded.

"Weren't you aware that he has advanced stomach cancer?"

"How advanced?"

"I'd give him a few weeks to a few months to live. I'm afraid there's nothing we can do."

"Can I see him?"

"Only for a short while. He's been given some powerful pain killers…strange that he didn't tell you. He received care in Helsinki and they put him on continuous pain medication…"

"Just a short while," said Raid.

The doctor led Raid into Nygren's room. It was small, and shared with five other patients. In between the beds were plastic curtains on casters. The doctor nodded and left.

Nygren seemed to be sleeping, but when Raid touched his hand, his eyes popped open.

"How you feeling?" asked Raid.

"Been better; just don't remember when."

"Why didn't you take your meds?"

"I thought I could do without. I couldn't. I gave up."

"Suppose you've given up on our trek, too."

"I didn't say that."

"What'd the doctor say?"

"Whatever he said, I'm getting outta here, and you're gonna help me."

"How?"

"Carry me out, for all I care."

The nurse peeked in the room and pointed at her watch. Raid nodded.

"Come back after midnight. There's nobody but nurses and an on-call doctor then. They won't be able to stop us," Nygren said.

"Are you sure about this?"

"Yes…but one thing."

"What?"

"The pain medication will wear off by early morning. I'll need more for the trip."

"I don't suppose aspirin would work."

"Morphine. I need morphine."

* * *

Raid came back just after midnight. He left the car as close as possible to the main entrance and studied the hospital for nearly ten minutes. Through the main glass doors, he could see the lobby, the receptionist and a couple of patients.

He left the car doors unlocked and walked straight inside, passed the receptionist and continued on toward Nygren's room. Before the receptionist realized what had happened, Raid was a ways off, and she ran after him.

"You have to sign in here," she said.

"I'm not a patient. I came to see my uncle."

"Clearly, visiting hours are over. The patients are asleep."

"Doctor Rimpinen called me. Said my uncle has only a few hours to live."

"He did? He didn't say anything to me…he's busy at the moment. What was the patient's name?"

"I know where he is."

Raid turned and walked off. This time, the woman didn't follow.

Nygren lay beneath the sheets, fully clothed, and upon seeing Raid, wrested himself upright. The lights woke up the patient in the adjacent bed and he began to mutter something about morning.

"It's not morning, go back to sleep," said Raid.

Nygren hung onto the edge of the bed and accustomed himself to being upright. He took a couple of trial steps and felt his vigor returning.

"Feels good, let's go."

"Sit down for a while. I'll go get some of that aspirin for you."

Raid headed down the hallway and stopped in front of a door on the left. The sign read, "K. Rimpinen." A sliver of light shone through the bottom of the door.

Raid opened the door to see K. Rimpinen enjoying a pastime he had apparently devised for the long hours of the night. A young nurse lay half-naked on the examination table. Her clothes were still on, but they were undone and raked aside. Her large breasts shuddered in time with Rimpinen's thrusting. The woman saw Raid first. She was so bewildered as to be speechless. His sudden entrance had ruined the moment and Rimpinen's enthusiastic efforts were going to waste.

"Good evening!" said Raid in a loud voice.

Rimpinen was so startled he nearly fell off the examination table. He tried to jerk his pants up, but had little success in a supine position. The nurse finally regained her faculties and pushed Rimpinen off.

Rimpinen got his pants up and patted his tousled hair back into place.

"Sorry, but your patient needs some pain killers,"

said Raid.

Rimpinen glanced at the nurse, who was wriggling her bra up her waist, then he followed Raid into the hallway.

"What patient…and who the hell are you?"

Then he remembered.

"You're Nygren's relative."

"He needs some pain medication for the trip. We'll be leaving shortly."

"The man is terminally ill. He can't go anywhere."

"Doesn't a dying man get to decide where to die?"

"We're talking about prescription pain-killers—they're extremely powerful drugs. I can't just hand them out to anybody."

Raid took a gun from beneath his coat and pressed it against Rimpinen's temple.

"Here's my prescription."

Rimpinen looked at the gun. It took a moment before he realized the delicateness of the situation.

"The pharmacy is on the second floor."

Raid followed him up the stairs. A sturdy-looking metal door barred the way to the pharmacy. Rimpinen took a large key out of his coat pocket.

"This is a serious crime, I hope you understand that."

Raid followed him into the pharmacy. The morphine and other powerful drugs were in a locked cabinet, and Rimpinen took out a second key.

"These come in tablets or in a liquid for syringes."

"Both."

Rimpinen took a box of both.

"The syringe," Raid demanded.

Rimpinen took a syringe and a box of needles off a shelf.

"Thanks."

Raid closed the door behind him and locked Rimpinen inside.

When he heard Raid's approaching footsteps, Nygren came out to join him. Together, they walked into the waiting room. Raid gave a wave to the receptionist, and by the time she was able to react, they were already outside.

"You rest in the back seat. We'll have to get as far as we can before they report us to the police."

"I won't slow us down. Step on it."

# 12.

When Lieutenant Kempas arrived at the physical rehab center, Jansson was suffering through one of the lectures. The topic was menopause and the accompanying psychophysical changes. Jansson could hardly believe his eyes when the speaker dug out a tube of personal lubricant, which had helped when her own secretions had started to dry up.

For once, Jansson was relieved to see Kempas.

"Sorry to interrupt such an interesting lecture."

They went to the cafeteria. Kempas bought a small coffee and brought it to a window table. He was dressed in a suit with a pinstripe pattern that was genuine 1960s vintage. The tie was wine-red with a small checked pattern.

Jansson almost felt pity for him. He knew Kempas was divorced, but even if he hadn't, he would have guessed. It was obvious that no woman had a say in what Kempas dressed himself in.

"I figured we'd better meet. I was in Kuopio and this happened to be on the way."

"Leino and Lunden were already here."

"That's not the same."

"I told them I haven't heard anything new."

"I wanted to hear it myself."

"Now you have."

"Why did Raid call you?"

"Just wanted to pass on a message."

"Right...that they wanna be left alone. Doesn't make sense. If they wanted to be left alone, why'd they blow off Sariola's fingers and a piece of his shoulder?"

"I didn't hear about that."

"Sariola's in the hospital in Kuopio. I went to see him but he's not talking...well...he is, but not enough."

"Where did the shooting happen?"

"At Nygren's place near Kuopio. The property is actually owned by one of his friends."

"What was Sariola doing out there?"

"He's not saying."

"Sariola and Leino already tried to pry some money out of Nygren. Doesn't it make sense that this was another attempt? They just bit off more than they could chew."

"It's possible."

"Is there a warrant out on Nygren?"

"Yes, for attempted murder. Same goes for Raid."

"Were there any witnesses?"

"Nope. We searched the place, but didn't find anything. A neighbor saw Nygren and Raid on the day of the shooting. He claims he doesn't know anything about it, but I could tell he was lying."

Kempas looked at Jansson expectantly.

"In other words, the situation has progressed quite a bit since we last talked. Do you think Raid will contact you again?"

"Hard to say."

Kempas watched a legless war veteran roll past the window.

"We've all lost something in this war. Some a leg, some an arm, some their soul…their future."

A text message appeared on Jansson's phone. He pulled it up on screen: *Need backup? Huusko.*

Jansson glanced around and spotted Huusko in the upstairs lobby. He tapped out a response: *Not yet.*

Kempas watched Jansson quietly as he did this.

"Are we on the same team here?"

"Yes," Jansson replied.

"Sure doesn't seem like it."

"No?"

"You have something against me?"

Jansson took a moment to consider why Kempas' attitude always sparked defiance in him. He decided not to answer.

"Do you know why people don't like me?" asked Kempas, his keen eyes seeming to burrow into Jansson's.

"What people?"

"My co-workers."

"I wouldn't say they don't like you."

"It's because I'm a cop 24-7. I'm serious about my work. Amateurs dislike professionals because they don't like to be reminded of what could be possible if they took their work seriously. Nobody wants to hear the truth."

"I do."

"Then you're in the same boat as I am…well over fifty and still a lieutenant while our captains and even their superiors are far less competent than we are."

"Being a captain doesn't interest me."

"That's exactly it. Do incompetent cops have to be

promoted just because they want to be?"

"You don't get ahead unless you want it."

Kempas ignored Jansson's comment.

"I've been in hundreds of department meetings, management seminars and training sessions. You wouldn't believe the trivial stuff they vacillate over, the way they dodge the truth and praise people who don't deserve it. If someone dares to tell the truth, everyone else is too afraid to listen. They plug their ears like little kids. The truth is too bitter a pill for most."

"What do you mean by 'the truth?'"

"That the entire system is based on praising worthlessness and incompetence. Competence and zeal are viewed as dangerous."

Kempas searched Jansson's eyes for support, but came up empty.

"Everyone thinks—maybe you do too—that I'm bitter because I haven't gotten further than I have. That's not it. I don't want to get any further. I'd rather solve one tough case right than wear a captain's stripes for the rest of my life. That's why I'm dangerous. And that's why I'm laughed at. The harder you laugh, the more they pat you on the back."

Jansson would have never imagined winding up as Kempas' confidante, especially not while sober.

"You're considered a good cop."

"I'm not asking for sympathy. I only want to be frank with you. I want us to agree on things."

"We do, in many respects," Jansson reflected.

"I respect your work and I hope you respect mine."

Something in Jansson's brain clicked into place and the truth dawned. The only reason Kempas was gushing was to soften him up. Kempas' methods exceeded all measures of crookedness by a long shot, but for some reason, Jansson was okay with it. He was almost pleased when he anticipated Kempas' next move.

"I need your help. If we can get Raid, we'll get Nygren too."

Kempas took a map out of his pocket. Here and there were red $x$'s, which he had jotted with a marker. He tapped the left lower corner with his finger.

"Turku. That's the first place Nygren and Raid went. We know he met a friend of his who runs a kind of makeshift church down there. From there they went northeast toward Kuopio."

He tapped on the next $x$.

"Here's where they first ran into Sariola and Lehto. Then they continued here to Nygren's place. That's where the trail ends."

Numerous red question marks also dotted the map.

"These indicate the homes of Nygren's past accomplices. Some have already been questioned."

Jansson glanced at the map. The northernmost question mark was in Lapland, near Rovaniemi.

"Where's Nygren from?"

Kempas pointed to the map.

"Somewhere around here."

"If he's saying his final farewells, you'd think he'd visit his childhood stomping grounds."

"Same thing occurred to me. The problem is that we're not sure where that is. By the time he was ten, he'd already lived in three different places."

"What about his daughter? He's got a grown daughter."

"I see we're on the same track. That also occurred to me."

Jansson's cellphone rang. The caller was Raid.

"Can you talk?"

"Hold on."

Jansson got up and withdrew from the table.

"They're after you guys for attempted murder."

"That's why I called. It was self-defense. Sariola shot first."

"You'd best come in with Nygren and explain."

"Can't do it."

"Why not?"

"Gotta take care of a couple things first."

"How long's that gonna take?"

"Couple days."

"There's a cop sitting about ten yards away who's after you and Nygren. He'll get a lot done in a couple of days."

"Tell him I said hello."

"Where are you?"

"Still hard to say."

"When will it be easy?"

"Be patient. You'll be the first to know. Trust me when I tell you we're doing the right thing."

"You forget that I'm a cop. You're asking too much."

"You forget that I'm a robber. I ask even more of myself. I'll call you tomorrow."

"That'd be best."

Jansson joined Kempas again.

"My wife. She's coming to visit on Saturday."

Kempas' expression didn't show whether or not he believed it. He was already on a new topic.

"When was the last time you ran into Nygren?" he asked.

"At least three years ago. Back when he was suspected of that bank robbery in Stockholm."

"You also investigated that casino shooting where Nygren was shot..."

"Been almost twenty years since then."

"When you questioned him in connection with the bank robbery, did he say anything new about the casino case?"

"If he didn't twenty years ago, why would he later on?"

"The case had exceeded its statute of limitations. He didn't have anything to fear anymore."

"He didn't say anything."

"Didn't mention any names?"

Jansson shook his head, unsure of what Kempas was getting at.

Kempas could see that Jansson wanted an explanation.

"I'm looking for names. I think Nygren's aiming to meet up with some old friends. I got a tip on the casino case..."

Anna was coming from the swimming pool with Huusko when Kempas fixed his eyes on her. As she turned to look at Jansson, she noticed Kempas. Suddenly, she turned on her heels and hurried away without a backward glance. Huusko looked confused for a moment before hurrying after her.

"What got into her?" wondered Jansson.

"Sometimes it scares me how much of an effect I have on women."

Jansson couldn't help laughing at the remark.

Kempas stood up, buttoned his coat and offered

his hand to Jansson.

"Thank you."

As soon as Kempas had left, Huusko appeared.

"Fuck, what a suit."

"What got into Anna?"

"Women. She remembered something important."

"What's the topic for the lecture this afternoon?"

"Viagra and other sex drive stimulants. Fifty plus only."

"You're lying."

"Yeah, I'm lying. Actually, it's much more interesting. The effect of fiber-rich foods on intestinal activity. Sixty plus only."

"You're lying."

"What do you want it to be then?"

"What's for lunch?"

"Rainbow trout casserole and zucchini au gratin. What'd Kempas want?"

"The same stuff."

"In other words…"

"You were there when Nygren was interrogated for the Stockholm bank robbery. Did he say anything about any old gigs?"

"All I remember is he was quite a riot. We had a hell of a laugh. The guy's had some pretty amazing exploits. This one time…"

"Huusko…the casino case."

"I don't remember him saying anything. Why?"

"Nygren was there gambling when the shooting happened. He was shot in the stomach and nearly died. I investigated it…"

"He didn't say anything."

"Kempas asked about it even though the case is ancient history."

"Why?"

"Something to do with a lead."

"If you investigated it, you should know better than I…who owned the casino?"

"Matti Salmi. We couldn't prove anything, but got some reliable tips. We never figured out who shot Nygren and the other gambler."

"What if they shot each other?"

"No weapons were found, and neither accused the other."

"Weren't there any other eye witnesses?"

"No…"

Jansson searched his memory.

"There was one… I think he was a maintenance guy. He heard the shots and saw the crowd pouring out of the casino. He was the one who called the ambulance…"

As Jansson rubbed his temples, the memories began to come back.

"We checked the maintenance guy's background, and it turned out he'd been in prison at the same time as Nygren. Because of that, we were suspicious of him, but found no evidence to indicate that he had anything to do with the casino."

Jansson took out his cellphone and punched one of the speed-dial numbers.

"Susisaari."

Susisaari's voice was always cool and businesslike, a potent tool for keeping client's emotions in check.

"It's me. Could you do me a little favor?"

"How little?"

"There are some files in the lower cabinet in my office. Find the one labeled, 'Casino Shooting.'"

"And?"

"There was a maintenance man who heard the shots and we interviewed him. Check the name, figure out where he lives and call me back."

"Is this urgent?"

"Not a matter of seconds."

"So ASAP."

"Right."

# 13.

Nygren was dozing in the back seat, looking utterly drained. Raid had given him a dose of morphine, but physical exhaustion wasn't his only problem. Raid could see from Nygren's eyes that the man's desire to surrender was beginning to triumph over the final special offers of life. Raid knew from experience how difficult it was to pull a man back once he understood how easy it would be to let go.

"You'll be back home soon."

Nygren perked up some. He hauled himself up, scooted over and all but pressed his face against the window.

"It's a long loop a man's gotta do before he gets back home."

"It's not over yet."

"The final leg, anyway."

As the town came into view, it seemed as though a theater curtain was opening. They passed through a deciduous forest and the hill dipped steeply toward a lake. Just beyond that was the town.

"Stop!"

Raid pulled the car to the side of the road and stopped.

Nygren gaped at the town in amazement.

"It looks almost the same. Has time come to a standstill?"

Raid glanced at his watch.

"Nope."

"When I left home at fourteen, I climbed up this very hill. I stood in this very spot and I looked back. I had my father's old rucksack, a pair of oversized pants and a pair of socks. My mom had stuffed some sandwiches and a vodka bottle full of milk into my bag. I was wearing a cap and had a harmonica I'd stolen from the neighbor boy in my pocket. Looking at the town from this hill, I had to fight back tears…but I was too stubborn to turn back…and here I am on the same path…"

A hint of a smile crossed Nygren's face and he looked at Raid.

"I never thought I'd fall for this sentimental bullshit."

"I'm happy to listen."

"Let's move."

The newer part of the town came into view on the far side of the hill, a strip mall and a few apartment buildings.

"Used to be fields where these are…the bridge seemed a lot bigger then…"

Raid stopped for a moment on the bridge.

"Always were lots of fish at the base of the pilings. Probably not anymore."

"Take a look."

Nygren glanced at him uneasily.

"Go see if there's fish. Then you won't be wondering."

"Well, why not."

Nygren rose from the car and walked to the

railing. Raid watched as he looked over. He stared into the water for a moment, then got back into the car.

"No fish…and just as well."

The streets of the old downtown were lined with large wood and stucco buildings.

"The bank, fabric shop, general store, book shop."

Nygren pointed to a fire station that was visible behind one of the wooden buildings.

"The school's behind the fire station."

Raid circled the building. Behind it was a Kingdom Hall for the Jehovah's Witnesses, but no school.

"They tore it down."

Nygren looked disappointed. His childhood memories had been stolen, and no one had told him.

"Let's go to the cemetery," said Nygren. "Unless they tore that down too."

Nygren navigated the walkways through long rows of graves. He seemed familiar with the place.

"The last time I was here was over thirty years ago when my father died. It was winter, almost thirty degrees below zero, and I didn't have a hat. I thought I was pretty cool. Everybody else was country folk, pretty much dressed in potato sacks. I was like a movie star from the big city. People were watching me and whispering… I enjoyed it."

A small front-end loader was digging a home for a new customer—a studio with eighteen square feet. Raid peered into the hole. The soil was ideal for digging, soft and yellow, but moist enough that it held together well. Tree roots hung from the sandy walls.

The wooden church was in the shape of a cross.

Nygren rounded it and headed toward the eastern end of the graveyard. He stopped near a low wall constructed of large boulders.

Just next to the wall was a squat, wide gravestone inscribed with two names:

Aini Sofia Nygren
Born 17.7.1911
Died 14.9.1953

Eero Veikko Nygren
Born 16.2.1907
Died 8.2.1970

The stone had been neglected and the names were hard to make out under the moss. The grass on the grave had been cut by the church, but there were no flowers. A shrub that had been planted at the grave a long time ago had died and its dried limbs jutted out of the ground.

"Mom and dad."

Nygren folded his hands and let them hang at his waist as if in prayer.

"A son visits his mother and father's grave for the first time in thirty-plus years and he doesn't even bring flowers."

A sprawling rose bush was growing on another grave a few yards away. Raid cut off a single rose and handed it to Nygren, who placed it on the grave.

"It's pretty easy to talk about death when you still have time. But when it's actually standing at your door, an inescapable fact of life, you forget the bullshit and all you have left is your fear. You can't think up a single smart-ass comment, even if your head was full of them before."

The gravedigger's shift was over. The drone of the front-end loader ceased.

"You just wonder if it hurts when a maggot burrows through your skull, and if you can see when your eyeballs dry into two gooey lumps…"

Nygren glanced at Raid.

"Pretty gruesome thought, huh? Sure, I could picture the flowers growing over me in the summer, the whispering winds rushing over me in the fall. And in the winter, I'll lie under a fresh white blanket of snow as lovers ski over my grave…"

"Right."

"There was a time when I was convinced I'd die with dignity. I pictured how calmly I'd watch the sunset and say, 'it's a good day to die.' Seemed so festive and beautiful that I almost looked forward to it."

"Aren't you convinced anymore?"

"I'm finally convincing myself that it won't be like that. That I'll whimper in terror and won't give a shit about dignity. I'll probably be bargaining with the devil for an extension."

Nygren looked at Raid inquiringly.

"Hard to say," said Raid.

"My mother had been dead for many years before I visited her grave for the first time. I pulled up the weeds around the grave and planted that shrub… An old woman stopped next to me and said, 'There's a fine resting place for a pious woman,' then smiled and walked away. Always kind of bothered me. I always wanted to know how she knew my mother. Were they classmates or something? One thing I'm sure of is that she wasn't speaking generally; by 'pious woman' she meant my mother... Mother was..."

Nygren became suddenly aware of his own words.

"We should get going."

On the left side of Nygren's parents' grave was a vacant strip with no headstone, but it clearly belonged to the same plot. Nygren noticed Raid looking at it.

"That one's mine."

Nygren's boyhood home was a good half mile from the church. Once past the church, the downtown area ended abruptly. Two-story wood and brick houses, some old, some new, drifted past on the roadside. They passed a small-engine repair shop, a dressmaker's shop, a bar and a pharmacy on the right. On the left, a 1970s white stucco school building loomed behind a sparse pine forest.

"The last time I drove this stretch there was no pavement," Nygren remarked. "No school, either. I had a fire-truck-red Porsche that I'd bought with some of the spoils from a gig. The way people stared at me, I should've pitched a tent and charged admission."

The roadside dwellings petered out for a while. On the right was a field, and on the left, a slope carpeted with pines.

Some modern row houses could be seen on the far side of the field.

The road climbed and curved gently to the right.

"Take a hard right at the top of the hill."

The road came to an end behind a pale-yellow house. A rusty van was parked in the yard.

"The addition wasn't there before...and the house was red."

Raid shut off the engine.

"The aspen's gone," Nygren noted.

"What aspen?"

"There was a big aspen growing over the root cellar. We had a fort there."

"You want to take a closer look?" asked Raid, but Nygren didn't seem to hear.

"The shed used to be on the left side of the house and the sauna was on the far end of the lot…"

Nygren fell silent and gazed at the yard.

"My mother planted the apple trees. I remember when she did it. She dedicated one tree to each child. The furthest one was Hanna's tree, Sylvi's is in the middle and mine is the closest to the house."

Nygren's tree seemed to be faring poorly. Some of its branches had dried and a few stunted apples hung in the canopy. The two other trees seemed to be growing well, with abundant fruit. The apples on the furthest tree were pale, and the other's were dark red.

Raid got out of the car and walked through the yard. A woman with a child in her arms was standing at the porch window. Raid waved and picked several apples from each tree. The woman opened the door and came out onto the stairs.

"Hello," said Raid.

She nodded stiffly, clearly frightened.

He took a twenty-euro bill out of his pocket and offered it to the woman.

"Six apples for a twenty. Fair?"

Raid left and the woman stood staring at the money in amazement.

Nygren studied the apples and smelled them with his eyes closed.

"I remember the smell."

He held the apple from his own tree in his palm. It was small, and some kind of apple blight had speckled it with black spots. He bit into it and grimaced, then opened the door and tossed it out.

"Let's go."

The town had only one hotel—a small inn in the old downtown. The lower level of the plastered brick building had once been home to a bank. Now it was occupied by the hotel's reception area and a restaurant. Upstairs were about ten rooms. Nygren had reserved two adjacent ones.

\* \* \*

Raid awoke to a scream just before three in the morning. It was followed by a broken howl and sobs, which faded almost completely before picking up again.

Raid threw on his pants, went into the hallway and opened Nygren's door with the key-card.

The light was on in the bathroom, and the open door cast a swath of light against the wall. Raid snapped on the lights in the entry. Nygren's room was identical to his own: a large bed, small nightstand, a television and a mini-bar. Raid's bar was still stocked, but Nygren's was empty. On the nightstand, rows of miniature bottles were arranged like chess pieces. Nygren's pants were neatly folded on the edge of the chair.

Nygren was sitting halfway up, and was staring blankly through his knees. His breathing was deep and labored. His hair jutted in every direction and his face glistened with sweat.

The only drink left was still in the mini-bar, an

unopened bottle of orange juice. Raid opened it, poured some into the glass on the nightstand and offered it to Nygren.

"You have a nightmare?"

Nygren raised his eyes. They were cloudy at first, but slowly he began to come out of it. His arms shuddered like they were freezing.

"No…it was hell."

He took the juice from Raid and gulped it down.

Raid opened the window and a southern breeze glided in along with the smell of fresh-cut hay.

Nygren crawled out of bed and went to the window. He put his head out and took a deep breath. His upper body was naked, his lower half clothed only in briefs. For his age, he was in good shape, slim and wiry. Only on his neck and face were the lines of age beginning to show. A thin gold chain with a small cross hung from his neck. A hawk flying skyward was tattooed on his right bicep.

"You wanna know what hell is like?"

"Not especially."

"It's a nightmare that ends in another that's even worse than the first, and the chain never ends. Your only emotion is fear, and every sense is harnessed for producing pain. In hell, you can't close your eyes or plug your ears, or take a gun and put a bullet through your head and say it's all over now. I thought I had rid myself of these dreams, but this was the worst one yet. Feels like my organs are on ice."

"You want something?"

"Just stick around long enough for my blood to start pumping again."

"Tell me about your dream."

"You don't wanna know."

"But you wanna tell."

Nygren snuffed out his cigarette and wrapped himself in a blanket.

"Well, I died…and, of course, with my lifestyle I ended up in the hot spot. These creatures were all over the place. The ones that, when I was a kid, used to jump out from underneath the bed when the lights were out. They surrounded me, kind of curious, and closing in the whole time. I tried backing up, but the ground was mucky and my feet were stuck. The first one that got to me stuck a sharp tongue out of its mouth, rammed it through me, and started eating my guts."

Nygren felt his stomach.

"Somehow I realized it was a nightmare and I forced myself to wake up, which I did, but only to another. I was standing out on the plains in Russia or somewhere. Not far off were some soldiers who looked like Huns hacking at their prisoners with these big sabers. Everything was in vivid detail, the soldiers' clothing, the horses' saddle ornaments, the fear in the dying men's eyes, the suffering. Everything seemed real.

"I was afraid the soldiers would notice me so I forced myself to wake up…"

Nygren gathered the blanket more tightly around himself. It seemed to Raid that Nygren was eyeing him warily, as if afraid he had woken up to yet another nightmare.

Raid lifted his hand and Nygren shrank away. Then he realized what Raid was up to and reluctantly touched his hand.

"Yarns from an old man."

Nygren took a cigarette off the table and lit it with

trembling fingers.

"Do you believe I'm not the least bit ashamed to admit that I'm afraid?"

"Yes."

"If you've done the kinds of things I have, and lived long enough, you're not capable of being ashamed of much anymore. At least not about what might matter to others. These days I'm only ashamed of stuff from the past."

Raid took a chair and sat down next to Nygren.

Nygren glanced at him.

"These memories keep coming back to me about things that happened decades ago. At the time, they didn't mean shit to me, but now I regret them, and I can't forget. They're like the bloodhounds of the past, tasked with chasing me to the grave. No matter how hard you try, you can't shake 'em off or bribe 'em."

Nygren beat his temple with the base of his palm, then glanced at Raid.

"Care to listen?"

Raid nodded.

"I was in my final year of elementary school when this family from the backwoods moved to town. They had nine kids. The dad got a job at the church as a gravedigger. He got drunk and dug graves. One winter he passed out at the bottom of the pit and got frostbite on his feet. One of the boys was in a lower grade than me, a short skinny kid with ratty clothes. One day he came to school with some new shoes, brand-new and squeaky clean, but damned if they weren't as long as canoes. You could just about spin 'em on his ankles. The kid's big brother was a couple years older and we heard from his friends that they took turns wearing the shoes. Every recess we picked on the kid and trampled on his toes. One time when we were teasing him, he took off the shoes and walked home in his socks. It was November and there was slush on the ground. He fell down once, but didn't give so much as a backward glance. Everyone else just stood there and watched as he walked away with his shoes in his hands. That was the last time he came to school and his family moved away soon after."

The memories weighed down on Nygren and he felt compelled to stand. He went to the window and took a breath of night air.

"The sad tale of the boy with big shoes—part two. When I was doing time in Oulu in the early eighties, I ran into him again. I found out he'd murdered two women he had just met at some Christmas party, and got life. There were lots of articles in the paper about it. One writer even sympathized with him...troubled childhood and so forth. I recognized him right away, but he didn't know who I was, nor was I too eager to reminisce about old times."

Nygren paused, "Well, tomorrow...today...is a busy day. I think I'll get some sleep."

Raid got up and Nygren stopped him.

"Thanks."

# 14.

"He hasn't been a father to me for over twenty years. A father is someone who lives with you, carries you on his shoulders, reads a bedtime story, tucks you into bed and kisses you goodnight. I was six when he left. The next time he saw us was two years later, and then again when I was confirmed. Since then I haven't even...and now you come asking about him as if I'd know."

"You're still his daughter."

"I have been the whole time, and he still hasn't come to visit."

Kempas was standing in the entryway and the woman seemed to have no intention of inviting him in. Some children's clothes hung from the hooks in the entry and several pairs of children's shoes and some blue rubber boots lay on the floor. Next to the wall was a telephone stand. From the entry, they could see a strip of the living room and a yellow sofa.

"Hasn't he met his grandchild?"

"Why are you asking about him? What'd he do this time?"

"We'd just like to chat with him about a certain case."

"By case you must mean a crime."

Nygren's daughter was thin and she had brown hair. Kempas could see Nygren's resemblance in her.

"Yes."

"I want to know what he's done."

"A man was shot and your father may have been involved."

"Did he die, this man?"

"No."

"He's not a violent man, you know."

"Who, your father?"

"Yes."

"We could use some coffee...it might be more comfortable to chat inside."

She wasn't going to be softened up that easily.

"I can't help you...and why would I? He's my father, after all."

"What do you do? For work, I mean."

"What does that have to do with anything?"

"I'm a policeman investigating a serious crime. Can't I indulge my curiosity a bit?"

"I work at a travel agency. Does that help?"

"You sell vacations?"

"Yeah."

"It's commendable when people do honest work. There'd be no need for us if everybody supported themselves with honest work. People who do honest work can help the police solve crimes. You have a child. Apparently a boy, judging by the color of those boots. How old?"

"Six."

"I want the world to be a better place for kids, including yours. That's why I'm a cop, and that's why I try to keep criminals from committing more crimes."

"My father might be a criminal, but he's not a bad person."

"When's the last time you saw him?"

"Am I being interrogated?"

"No. You can refuse to talk or you can lie. But I hope you don't."

The woman bowed her head. She took a moment before making her decision.

"A few days ago."

"Where?"

"Here…in the yard. He was just passing through and came to see me…only for a couple minutes. He didn't even come inside."

"Where was he headed?"

"He said north to Lapland, nothing more."

"What did he want?"

"I think he just wanted…wanted to see me…and his grandchild."

"What did you discuss?"

"We didn't talk much…he apologized for being a terrible father… Read a poem and left."

"Read a poem?"

"He wrote a poem about me when I was little. He had saved it and gave it to me."

"What else?"

"He told my son he's going to Lapland and he'll say hi to Santa Claus…then he left…"

Kempas scrutinized the woman's every aspect, the movements of her eyes, the wrinkles in her brow, her hand gestures.

"Is there anything else?" said Kempas. He always asked the question just to be sure. It had scored him many bonuses. This time he knew there was something more.

"He left me…gave me some money…"

"Money? How much?"

"Twenty thousand euros."

"Oh!" Kempas breathed. "A large sum. Did he say where it came from?"

"He just left a package that I didn't open till I got inside. I thought it was a toy for Jari…otherwise I wouldn't have taken it."

"Was there anything else in the package?"

"A note."

"What kind of note?"

"It was a message…for me…"

"Yeah?"

"It said…that he loves me…"

The woman's voice cracked. She covered her eyes with her hand.

Kempas put his hand gently on her shoulder.

"You've been a huge help. I only have a couple more questions…if it's alright."

She wiped her eyes and composed herself. Kempas didn't hurry her.

"Did he leave any contact information? An address, a phone number or a name?"

The woman shook her head. She kept sniffling and she wiped her eyes again.

"Do you know if he has any acquaintances or relatives up north?"

"No, and if he does I don't know them. We're not exactly a close family."

"What about his ex-wife, your mother?"

"She lives in Espoo. I doubt he's been in contact with her. She called yesterday and she certainly would have said something."

"Did you tell her that Nyg…your father came?"

"Yes."

"What did she say?"

"That it was just like my father to drop by unannounced for five minutes and take off."

Kempas thought for a moment. The sweatband of his hat was damp and his scalp began to itch. He scratched at his hairline. Some dandruff dropped onto the shoulders of his coat and stood out clearly against the black fabric.

"What should I do with the money?"

"Where is it?"

"It's here…I haven't spent any…"

"Spend it however you deem fit. We're not aware of the money being linked to any crimes."

"You mean…can I really…"

Kempas raised his right hand in the scout's oath.

"Cops don't lie. You've got my permission to spend it."

She smiled for the first time.

"One more thing. Was he alone?"

"No."

"Was he accompanied by a man named Raid?"

She nodded.

"Did this Raid say anything?"

"No. Not a word."

"We'd like to know more about him…especially how your father knows him."

The woman looked at Kempas, somewhat surprised.

"You mean you don't know?"

\* \* \*

Nygren's daughter's apartment was on the fourth floor. Kempas decided to take the stairs down, though the elevator had already been waiting.

The yard and playground were visible from the windows in the landings. A group of boys had gathered to build a race track in the sandbox. Kempas walked over to watch them play.

"Is one of you Jari?"

A boy with a ball cap looked up.

"Are you Jari?"

"Yeah."

"How'd you like to help me out with a top secret detective case?"

"What case?"

Kempas took out his badge.

"Do you know how to read?"

"Yeah...I'm in kindergarten."

"What's it say here?"

The boy studied the word and sounded it out.

"Po...pol...police...you're really a policeman?"

"Sure. I'm gonna ask you a couple of detective questions...should we go over there? To the swings?"

Kempas settled into a swing. The boy hesitated before hopping onto the neighboring one.

"Your grandpa stopped by a few days ago, isn't that right?"

"Yeah...he promised to say hi to Santa."

"Did your grandpa give you anything?"

"No, but he said he'd ask Santa to give me something. Grandpa said he's good friends with Santa."

"Did grandpa say where he was going?"

"To Santa's workshop."

"Did he say anything else?"

"No…I'm not sure I like grandpa…he made my mommy cry…"

"Mommies do that sometimes."

The boy beamed. "But the good thing is he's really rich."

"I guess so…do you know how to use the telephone?"

"Yeah, that's easy."

"Let's make a secret pact. If your grandpa sends you a card or a present, call me right away. I'll give you some police stuff as a reward."

"A gun?" the boy perked up.

"Well, not quite, but something really cool. What would you think about handcuffs? You could catch criminals with 'em, right?"

"Yeah! I want some handcuffs!"

Kempas underlined the cell number on his business card and handed it to the boy.

"But don't tell your mom. You're never supposed to tell moms about secret pacts."

# 15.

A man stepped out of a black 1970s Cadillac and glanced around. Under forty, his short hair had been dyed blond and a gold ring pierced his right ear. His black trench coat seemed too tight and he walked with his arms akimbo like a body builder. Though the sidewalk was bustling with traffic, he lumbered through unhindered.

"Rusanen is paranoid. He's afraid the cops are following him," said Nygren as he observed the man through binoculars from the back window of the Mercedes.

"I'm afraid of that, too," said Raid.

"They're not. I know."

"How?"

"I read it in the horoscopes."

The man loitered around, shifting from spot to spot and glancing this way and that. He had been doing the same routine for ten minutes, despite the drizzling rain. On one occasion, he had stopped to sit for a couple of minutes in his black Cadillac.

The Mercedes was far enough away that there was no danger of being discovered.

"Go inside already, we don't have all day," Nygren muttered to himself.

The man made his decision and headed toward a moss-green two-story job site trailer. The trailer sat within a fenced-in storage area full of scaffolding, dismantled cranes, pallets, rusty piles of rebar and concrete tubes. Just next to the fence was a gray metal pole building. The drizzling rain only highlighted the grunginess of the area.

"The construction company is owned by a dummy firm, just like everything else of Rusanen's."

"Let's go."

Raid started the engine and pulled up to the spot the body builder had just vacated.

Nygren got out of the car and Raid followed.

"You sure about this?"

"Yes. This is no whim."

Raid nodded and headed toward the trailer. Just in front of it was a blue Volvo, which had already been there when Raid and Nygren had come by earlier to check out the trailer. Despite the parked Volvo, nobody but the blond muscle man with the gold earring was in the trailer.

Raid opened the door and stepped inside. The trailer was furnished like an office. Shelves lined the walls, and in front of the windows were two desks littered with blueprints and binders. The man was filling the coffeemaker by the sink.

He turned to face Raid.

"Hello," Raid said.

The man stared silently back at Raid.

"You need a hard worker?"

"You're in the wrong place. Beat it."

When Raid didn't move, the man came up to him and jabbed him in the chest with his thick forefinger.

"What are you some fucking idiot?"

"My friend wants to talk to you."

"What friend?"

"An old one."

"Tell your friend to come inside…you stay out there."

Raid stepped back a ways.

"Are the cops watching this place?"

"If they are, they are. What's it to me?"

Raid knocked on the window and Nygren came in.

The man recognized him immediately.

"Nygren!"

"Rusanen."

Rusanen weighed his options. Nygren was a worthy opponent. It wouldn't be wise to make him mad.

"What brings you to Oulu?"

"Just passing through."

"And you just stumbled on this place, right? Bullshit."

"Maybe a little bird told me."

"If you got something to say, say it. I'm busy."

"I came to speak on behalf of the boys. You're treating them poorly."

"Then the door's right over there. If they have something to say, they can say it themselves… Probably was Hiltunen who came bawling to you…"

"No names."

"That pussy needs a little straightening out."

"No, you do."

Rusanen looked as if he'd been pumped up to 100 PSI. He restrained himself for a moment before exploding.

"Goddamn asshole, go fuck yourself!"

"I wish I could."

"You got about ten seconds before I toss your ass out."

Rusanen glanced at his flashy watch. Judging by the sparkles, it must have been studded with either gold and diamonds or cheap baubles.

Nygren watched him coldly.

"How much time left?"

Rusanen reached for the desk and snatched up a kitchen knife that he had been slicing bread with.

"None."

He advanced on Nygren, brandishing the knife like they did in the movies. In real life, of course, the Hollywood approach rarely works. Raid let him gesticulate a while. In his rage, the man had forgotten that Nygren was not alone.

Raid took out his gun and leveled it at the man's forehead.

"Enough."

The man glanced to the side and saw the gun. His knife hand froze in the striking position.

"Two against one and you still need a gun?" blurted muscles.

"You promised to teach Hiltunen a lesson, and I promised to teach you one, so which of us will keep his word?" said Nygren.

"Have us two ever had a problem?"

"We do now."

"If Hiltunen's running his mouth, he's gotta learn his lesson. What if someone was talking behind your back?"

"You won't be giving any more lessons. You won't exist anymore."

Rusanen took a conciliatory slant.

"If you have a bone to pick with me because of

your cellmate, then let's just say it was a mistake, a complete accident."

"You're a complete accident."

"Let's do this…how 'bout I bring you into the business. You get a slice of everything. Everyone wins, and no hard feelings."

Nygren held out his hand and Raid handed him the gun.

Nygren aimed it at the space between Rusanen's eyes. Rusanen could see this was no bluff.

"There's twenty grand in the safe. Take it and get out."

When Nygren didn't respond, Rusanen swallowed hard.

"Don't try to play all innocent. Everyone knows what you've been up to. Sariola says you stiffed him."

"Is that what Sariola says?"

"I'm just telling you what he said. I don't necessarily believe him. You got a reputation of being fair. Twenty grand up front and you get a cut of the profits. I got good contacts with Russia, Holland and the States. You'll get a better return on that than any fucking tech stocks."

"Not interested. The outlook isn't so good for your business."

"What, then? Tell me and we can iron things out. Have some coffee… There's Cognac in the cabinet. Let's have a few shots and talk about old times."

"I'll serve the shots."

Nygren waved the pistol.

Rusanen tried to make a joke of it, which fell flat: "So you wanna make the cops happy?"

"And myself, and many others."

Raid went to the window and peered out. He looked back and nodded.

Nygren pulled the trigger. The bullet hit Rusanen in the forehead and he keeled over against the sink and flopped onto the floor.

Raid took the gun out of Nygren's hand.

"Let's go."

Nygren blinked as though awakened from a dream.

"We'll need a head start. We gotta ditch the body."

Nygren couldn't stop staring at it. Raid got a tarp from the storage building and wrapped up the body. They carried it to the edge of the property and heaped a pile of pallets and some other trash on top of it.

After that, Raid drove straight back to the highway and turned north. Nygren sat on the back seat, completely silent.

# 16.

Jansson was awaiting his wife's arrival with equal parts anticipation and trepidation. His conscience nagged at him, though he had only done it with Anna in his dreams, if even that.

Jansson was particularly afraid of running into Anna with his wife. If he behaved differently, his wife would notice.

And even if she didn't, Anna was the kind of woman who could stir unease in any wife, even his own.

After breakfast, Jansson went for a swim. He swam over twenty laps. Afterwards, he stopped into the weight room to bend, lift, pull and pedal with various devices to build muscles that he had never known he had.

Jansson liked the fact that there were no instructors on the weekends and he could toil away as he saw fit. Besides himself, the only other person in the gym was Huusko.

"The only exercise we're missing is the one for your sphincter," Huusko commented.

Huusko sat on the pec deck working his shoulder and pectoral muscles. He did twenty reps at a brisk pace.

"Still homesick?"

"Two weeks here is too long."

"True. One week would've been plenty, now that I think of it."

"The wife's coming to visit," said Jansson.

"She's in for the shock of her life."

"How so?" Jansson wondered.

"When her trim detective lieutenant and his love shuttle toss her onto the sheets and lead her to the seventh heaven of lust."

"Huusko, has anyone told you how tasteless your jokes are?"

"Yes. You have yourself many times."

Jansson didn't ordinarily pay Huusko's banter any mind. He knew Huusko didn't intend any harm, nor good for that matter—he didn't intend anything. According to his own personal credo, he had to find the humorous side in everything, or at least humorous to him. On the other hand, banter was Huusko's way of showing that he and Jansson were good friends. Among good friends, you could throw insults around without cause for anger. And the ribbing was always dispensed in a humorous way, not in a hurtful one.

"Did they measure your legs?" Huusko asked.

"What do you mean?"

"Not joking. Lopsided legs lead to back pain so they measure everybody. So it was my turn yesterday, and turns out my left leg is a quarter-inch shorter than the right. I've been leaning left my whole life and only now do I figure out why."

"So what's the treatment for lopsided legs…a doctor?"

"A shoemaker. My left shoe needs a thicker sole."

"Wouldn't it be easier to just leave the right shoe off?"

A veteran who was missing his right arm and left leg came into the gym. He went to the upright rowing machine and started hoisting the weights into the air with his one hand.

Huusko climbed onto the stationary bike and started pedaling.

"Have you heard from Raid?"

"No."

"You're not too thrilled about helping Kempas catch Nygren."

"I'll help if there's a reason."

"You don't think Nygren and Raid are up to anything?"

"Of course they're up to something, but not what Kempas has in mind."

"What, then? Raid didn't say?"

"No."

"You trust him more than Kempas?"

"In this instance."

Jansson's cellphone rang. The caller was Sergeant Susisaari.

"This a bad time?" she asked.

"I'm on an exercise bike."

"Can you steer with one hand?"

"Yes, and talk at the same time."

"You guys never cease to amaze me… We got a call from the Oulu PD. A local crime boss was found dead, and they suspect Nygren and Raid are involved."

"Why?"

"Why was he shot or why are they suspects? That was a joke. Because someone saw an old Mercedes near the crime scene."

Huusko had climbed off the bike and was listening in.

"What kind of a crime boss are we talking about?"

"Big time drug-dealer. They suspect he controls the drug traffic in all of northern Finland. Used to own a gym...extremely violent."

"Has Nygren had anything to do with this guy?"

"Supposedly they did time together in Oulu."

"And Raid?"

"As far as I know they hadn't met. Oulu PD asked for your help since you know both Raid and Nygren. They're afraid a gunfight could break out when they arrest those two so they might need a negotiator. I promised you'd call either way. Lieutenant Jaatinen is leading the case...you know him?"

"I do. Anything else?"

"You asked about that maintenance guy from the casino shooting. Name's Keijo Hiltunen. Lives in Rovaniemi."

Jansson memorized the address she gave him. Rovaniemi, Finland's gateway to the arctic, was only about 150 miles north of Oulu.

"Thanks."

"How's it going over there?"

"Might be bulking up a bit too much."

"And Huusko?"

Huusko heard his name being mentioned and pressed his ear up against the phone.

"Completely wiped out. Would've never expected it from someone that young."

"Say hi for me."

"I will."

Jansson hung up and turned to Huusko, "You get

all that?"

"Enough. God will reward my good deeds. I got an idea."

"Do tell."

"We got an excuse to get outta here now. As good cops, how could we turn down an official request for backup? The boys up north need our help finding Nygren and Raid."

"How we gonna do that?"

"We'll have time to think about it on the way to Oulu."

Jansson went into the locker room and called home. He caught his wife just as she was leaving.

"Will you be disappointed if we can't meet up?"

"Of course I will. What happened, you find a sexier date?"

"No such thing."

"That'll earn you some points."

"We got a call from Oulu. A murder case."

"Is that what they're called nowadays?"

"I know the suspects and…"

She interrupted him.

"I was just kidding. Of course you'll go, as long as they let you come back."

Huusko snuck into the locker room.

"I figured I'd come straight home then," said Jansson.

"As long as you let me know ahead of time so I can shoo off all the young bucks."

"I promise I will."

"Drive safely."

"Huusko's driving."

"Then no point in saying anything to him. You know, I had some plans in store for you. I bought some lingerie…black and naughty."

"Thanks. I'll enjoy those when I get home."

"Nonsense. I bought them for myself."

"Nonsense. You're the love of my life."

"That's enough. You're getting a little too sappy."

"True."

After saying goodbye, Jansson hung up.

Huusko was cramming his things into a tattered gym bag.

"You two always talk like that?"

"Usually."

"With all that sweet talk, you're lucky you don't have diabetes. When do we leave?"

"Right away."

Jansson went into his room to pack. He had just gotten his things into his suitcase when the phone rang. It was Raid.

"We agreed that I'd call if something happens."

"Yes?"

"Something happened."

"What?"

"Someone died."

"You killed him?"

"No."

"Nygren did?"

"Yeah."

"Were you with him?"

"Tough to say."

"You talking about a guy from Oulu by the name of Rusanen?"

"Good guess."

"Nygren's car was seen near the crime scene. I'm leaving for Oulu right now to look into it. They're looking for you two."

"I know. We should meet."

"Where are you?"

"I'll call you back this evening."

"You promised you wouldn't do anything I wouldn't do."

"And I haven't."

"Nygren has."

"Not as far as I'm concerned."

"Are we talking self-defense?"

"In a way."

"In any case, you've gone too far."

"If you knew Rusanen, you'd have done the same."

"I doubt it."

"One more request."

"What?"

"I'll tell you when I see you. I'll call later."

Huusko appeared at the door with his bag. Jansson grabbed his brand-new Samsonite suitcase.

"This is the last time you talk me into coming here," said Jansson.

In the parking lot, Anna hurried over to them.

"Do you have a minute?" she asked Jansson.

Huusko snuck sheepishly into the car. Jansson edged a little further away.

"What is it?" said Jansson.

"I don't want you to have the wrong impression of me. I wasn't flirting with you to get you to do something for me. I did it because I like you. You seem so…safe."

Jansson didn't reply.

"What did that cop, Kempas, say about me?" she asked.

Jansson recalled her sudden departure after she

had caught sight of Kempas.

"Do you know him?"

"I could tell he wasn't saying anything nice."

"He didn't say a single word about you."

Anna didn't seem to hear.

"Everywhere you look, there's spiteful people spreading gossip and lies."

"He wasn't talking about you," Jansson repeated.

Anna leaned in and kissed Jansson on the cheek.

"Maybe another time," she whispered.

"Maybe," Jansson caught himself muttering.

Anna turned and headed off toward the main building.

Jansson got in the car.

"She sure was lovey-dovey," said Huusko.

"Shut up."

Huusko was surprised by Jansson's glare, and he bit his tongue.

# 17.

Raid turned onto a side road and came to a stop in a sparse pine forest. He peeled the wrapper off a disposable syringe and loaded it with a dose of morphine. Nygren had wrapped his arms around himself and was holding on as if fearful of falling apart. Raid pressed him against the seat so he could inject the morphine.

The pain had returned a couple of hours earlier, but Nygren had stubbornly resisted until it overpowered him. His face pale and damp, he had asked Raid to drive to a secluded spot.

The morphine took effect rapidly and Nygren's pained expression softened.

Raid offered him a carton of orange juice. Nygren drank the whole thing.

"Feel better?"

The color began to return to Nygren's face.

"Seems rather unfair that at my age and with my history, I'm forced to realize I'm not as tough as I had imagined."

"You don't have to prove anything to anybody."

"I do. To myself. You can fool others, but not yourself, at least I can't. And I don't think you can either."

"True."

"Let's get going, then. I'd like to sleep in clean sheets tonight."

Raid started the car and drove back to the main road. Nygren settled into the back seat in a semi-reclining position and stared out the window.

"How are you feeling?" Raid asked.

"Brittle as a cracker."

This most recent bout had sapped Nygren's energy for the past twenty-four hours. At the outset, he had slept for almost ten hours. After awakening, he had kept to himself in the back seat. Raid almost missed his constant chit-chat.

"You never finished the story about this car."

"You really wanna hear it?"

"Sure. If you have the energy."

Nygren considered whether he wanted to tell it, and whether Raid wanted to listen. "I think you really wanna hear it."

"Let's hear it."

Nygren struggled to sit up a bit more.

"I think I left off with the rich farmer who had bought the car from a widow. The car had been in the farmer's garage almost ten years, and he couldn't bring himself to drive it but a few times, as stingy as he was. He normally drove a twenty-year-old piece of shit Nissan. In the end, he didn't get to enjoy the car much. Death came and reaped itself a frugal, greedy man. Inevitably, the old maxim held true: you can't take your mammon to hell with you, not even a Mercedes."

"Ladas are allowed, though."

Nygren glanced at Raid, somewhat confused.

"Don't they drive Ladas in the Mercedes-man's

hell?" Raid continued.

Nygren's cackle turned into a cough. He hacked and barked until his lungs were clear.

"And as it often goes in this just world of ours, the money and riches go to those who don't work up a single drop of sweat for it. The man had a punk kid who'd dropped out of school and was living off his old man's money. Since he was the guy's only son, the farm and car went to him."

The sun began to set and an orange fan of light spread out in the western sky. The pines lining the road were flushed in the evening sun.

"I had just taken care of a small deal in Rovaniemi and I stayed the night at the Hotel Pohjanhovi. The kid was there with his entourage. He fancied himself quite the card shark and was looking for a game. I happened to have ten grand in loose change in my pocket."

"And you won the car," Raid guessed.

Nygren shot him a dour look.

"If someone's telling you a story, you don't spoil it by trying to guess the ending."

"Sorry."

"We played all night. As the hours ticked by, the others dropped off one by one, but the kid had serious bread. By six in the morning, he'd lost all his money and was eight grand in debt. He learned the hard way that the world can be a tough place."

"Did you cheat?"

"Don't interrupt. We agreed that we'd sleep a few hours and then meet in the downstairs lobby at noon…"

With obvious difficulty, Nygren dug a pack of cigarettes out of his pocket and lit one with his old

Zippo. He took a drag and blew the smoke toward the roof of the car, took a couple more drags and flicked the cigarette out the window.

"I think I'm finished…smoking."

Nygren looked at Raid. Raid nodded.

"It was a joke."

"I got it."

"Everything comes to an end eventually."

"You didn't finish your story."

"Maybe you were listening after all… When I arrived at the meeting place, the kid was nowhere to be seen. I asked the receptionist and found out that he and his cronies had taken off at the crack of dawn. Lucky for me he was easy to find. Everyone knew the local lowlife and prodigal son. I had to use a bit of force to get into the house. The guy was holed up in the upstairs bedroom, taking a nap in his daddy's chippendale bed with the silk sheets and all. I woke him up a little rough and knocked him upside the head a few times, but he claimed he didn't have any money at the moment. Supposedly, he had to liquidate some assets. At the time, I didn't have a car, so I asked him if he did. He had two: a Porsche and this. I took the Mercedes. It's been seven years already and the car has served me faithfully."

"Interesting story, but did you cheat?"

"The story is educational, too," Nygren went on, oblivious to Raid's question.

"You must think I need a little education," Raid said.

"Everybody does."

"Right."

"What do you know about women, for example?" Nygren asked.

"I'm a big boy now."

"Every man thinks he knows everything about women, even if he can barely manage a bra strap. A woman can make heaven or hell of a man's life, or both at the same time. I'd advise you to treat the matter with the seriousness it demands."

"I do."

"If you did, you'd have a woman."

"I have."

"But not anymore."

"That's a question of interpretation. Do you have one?"

"Don't do as I do, do as I say."

"How many times have you been married?"

Nygren counted on his fingers.

"Three."

"You didn't treat the matter with the seriousness it demanded."

"That's right. The first lasted six years, the second and third were under a year. I shouldn't even count the third. She was a prison shrink and far more in need of help than I was. Criminals don't make good husbands."

"True."

"I'm almost sixty years old—you're about half that. Based on my age, I've got twice your life experience, and I'm willing to pass it on to you. You should get it for free while you can. Ask me whatever you want."

"Where we sleeping tonight?"

"In a hotel."

"What are we doing here?"

"Meeting an old friend of mine."

Raid turned his eyes back to the road.

"That's all your questions? A sorry showing. My forte is the meaning of life. In prison there was plenty of time and a good library for those who wanted to exercise something other than their criminal instinct. Have you read Primo Levi's *If This Is a Man*?"

"No, but I've read Shakespeare's *Moby Dick*."

"What about Twain's 'Captain Stormfield's Visit to Heaven?'"

"No, but I've read Adam Smith's *The Communist Manifesto*."

Nygren was undeterred by Raid's wisecracks.

"You're stubborn, just like when you were a little boy. Haven't you learned how to take advice yet?"

"Let's have it."

"Read. Reading is the shortcut to everything. A book is like a little package with generations of wisdom on the meaning of life."

"You don't think I read?"

"Do you?"

"Of course I do."

"What did you mean when you said that whether you were dating was a question of interpretation?"

"Just that."

"I've certainly heard more intelligible expressions. Either you have a woman or you don't. Which is it?"

"None of your business."

"So that's how it is?"

"First tell me if you cheated that kid."

"Yes, but I didn't need to. He was a pitiful gambler. Now your turn."

"There's a woman...she's waiting for me."

"Is she a good woman?"

"Yes."

"What's she do for a living? Not that it makes a difference…"

"It doesn't."

"I can almost guess how you met."

"You guessed right."

"How long has she had to wait?"

"Six months."

"Have you been in contact?"

"I sent a card."

"Just one?"

"Just one."

"If she waits for you, hold onto her. One card isn't a lot."

"Right."

"Does she know what you do?"

"Yes."

"And she's still waiting? Again, hold onto that one."

"You might know her dad."

"Do I?"

"If you know Uki."

"Uki?"

"Yeah."

"*The* Uki?"

"Yeah."

"Small world…too small. Uki helped me out with a job once. Opened a door for me…the door to a safe. A real professional. And you're dating his daughter? Hold onto that girl, but keep your distance from her dad. That's my free advice for you."

* * *

Nygren gave directions as he studied the map.

"Go right at the next intersection. Then left. There's the sign right there."

Raid pulled into a combination gas station, auto repair shop, and small bar. The 1960s building was clad in white asbestos shingles, some of which had cracked. Nygren took a look around. Signs of decay were apparent elsewhere as well.

"Doesn't look like much," Raid said.

A young man in his twenties was tending the register. His long hair was tied back in a pony tail.

"Hiltunen? Is he here?" Nygren asked.

The young man appraised the visitors before answering.

"Back in the shop. I'll get him."

"Thanks, but we can find him."

Dressed in blue overalls and a cap, Hiltunen stood inspecting the radiator of a car that was parked over the service pit. Nygren had to clear his throat to get the man's attention.

"Hello," said Nygren.

"Nygren!"

Hiltunen's age was difficult to gauge. He was small and dreary. His brown eyes were bright and friendly, but tinged with worry. Raid suspected that he and Nygren were to blame for that.

"We were on our way north to buy some reindeer antler tonic and I figured we'd stop and say hi."

Hiltunen was hardly overjoyed.

"Where'd you get this address?"

"From a friend. You have time for coffee? My treat."

Hiltunen hesitated briefly before accepting the invitation.

Hiltunen kept his coveralls and cap on. He tore some paper towels off a roll and wiped down his shoes, which were brand-new and gleaming, hardly a match for his coveralls.

Outside, the wind drove the rain across the pavement. The gas pumps were sheltered by a small canopy, which provided little cover now. A woman filling up her car lost her hat, which rolled across the parking lot and under a parked van.

Hiltunen was wrapping up a summary of the years since his prison release.

"...so I've been managing this place for about seven years. The owner's retiring and means to sell the place. We'll see what happens to me. I'm old enough now that it looks like I'll end up on unemployment."

"How's business?"

"Not so bad, though you wouldn't believe that by lookin' at it. The owner's just too stingy to fix it up. The location's good. If he'd just invest a little in the repair shop and spruce it up a bit things would get better. My boy's a good mechanic...been working with cars since he was a little kid."

Hiltunen nodded at the young man behind the register.

"That him?"

A look of fear crossed Hiltunen's face, as though he had revealed too much.

"Yeah."

"How's your wife?"

"Working in the hospital kitchen... What about you?"

"Retired."

Hiltunen glanced at Raid from beneath the brim of

his cap and Nygren noticed.

"That's my nephew. He's my chauffeur and tour guide. We're headed to Lapland. You ever thought of buying this place for yourself?"

"With what money? With my record, I can't get a loan without serious equity."

"How much do you need?"

"What do you mean?"

"I could give you loan."

Hiltunen shook his head.

"Nothin' against you, but I don't wanna get mixed up in anything. Been tryin' to stay clear of ex-cons, no matter how nice they are…"

"What about Rusanen?"

"What about him?"

"You working for him?"

"Some small gigs… I got to…"

"Not anymore."

"How's that?"

"He's dead. He was shot yesterday."

"Can't be…"

"He is."

"Best news I've heard all day…see that in the paper?"

"No, but word travels."

"It's about time someone put him out of his misery… I thought about it myself, but wasn't man enough."

"About my offer, maybe you misunderstood. I don't want to interfere with your life, just want to loan you some money."

"How come?"

"You have to invest your money somewhere. A reasonable interest rate would suffice."

"What's reasonable interest?"

"Five percent."

"Fifty grand. I can get the rest from the bank."

"Is that enough?"

"It'll have to be."

Nygren held out his hand, "Deal?"

"What kinda money is this?"

"From my retirement account."

"What about collateral?"

"Make the place profitable. That's all the collateral I need."

Hiltunen was dumbfounded.

"Deal?" Nygren asked again.

Hiltunen decided to risk it. He couldn't think of anything in the proposal that could worsen his current predicament.

"Deal."

"The money will be in your account tomorrow."

Nygren gulped down the rest of his coffee and got up.

"Thanks for the coffee. We'll be on our way."

Hiltunen walked them out to the car. He took off his cap and offered his hand to Nygren.

"Thank you."

Nygren shook his hand.

Hiltunen shook hands with Raid as well.

As they drove away, Hiltunen stood in the middle of the lot and beheld his future domain. He stood so straight he seemed four inches taller than when Raid and Nygren had arrived. Raindrops pattered onto his slick shoes, and with nothing to cling to, they slid onto the concrete.

* * *

Nygren sat in the back seat reading a tabloid. His mood was buoyant.

"Who is this Hiltunen?" asked Raid.

"Someone I met in prison."

Raid drove for ten minutes without saying a word. Nygren folded the paper and set it aside on the seat.

"You're wondering who he is?"

"Yeah."

"Hiltunen's the boy with the too-big shoes."

# 18.

Jansson and Huusko arrived in Oulu at about six in the evening. On the way, Huusko had broken the speed limit about a hundred times. Actually just once—for the entire trip.

Jansson was bothered by the fact that they had abandoned the rehab center. He felt like a fugitive with a stiffer sentence in store once he was recaptured. Huusko didn't seem a bit bothered.

"Don't worry about anything today that you can worry about tomorrow," Huusko said.

To Jansson's surprise, Huusko disclosed a bit from his closely-guarded past.

"Once when I was about ten, I had to go to a summer camp with my brother, but all I ever wanted was to spend the summer in town with my buddies. After a week, I'd got my fill of homemade yogurt, barley flour, and dill beef stew, so a friend and I decided to run off. We only made it a few miles before getting caught. Ended up thumbing a ride from the camp director. The guy was so crafty he'd taken somebody else's car so we wouldn't recognize it. This has the same feel to it."

The Oulu police station was on Railway Square, in the heart of the city. Huusko parked hastily next to a squad car. He tugged up the squeaky emergency brake and was out of the car in no time.

Jansson was tired and dazed, even though he'd been napping most of the trip. He climbed stiffly out of the car and bent over to get his jacket out of the back seat.

They rang the door buzzer and the door clicked open. Jaatinen, the lieutenant in charge of the Rusanen murder investigation, was waiting in an upstairs conference room. The table was set with coffee and sandwiches. A couple members of Jaatinen's team were also there. Everybody shook hands.

"We'll be getting a few more of you guys shortly," said Jaatinen.

"What do you mean 'more of us?'" said Jansson.

"Lieutenant Kempas and a couple other men from Helsinki. Kempas called and told us they've been trailing these guys for some time. They left Kuopio a couple hours ago so they should get here by eight or nine."

"Super," said Huusko.

Jaatinen detected the insincerity in his voice.

"Is there something I should know?"

"Nah, inside joke."

"Not many insiders in your circle, then."

Jaatinen gestured toward his two men.

"Here's my own inner circle, Sundell and Heikkilä."

Sundell poured everyone coffee and passed a sandwich tray around. Huusko took a ham sandwich and Jansson settled on a croissant.

"I'm glad you guys could make it. If it turns out our two suspects are the actual shooters, we're in for quite the chase. I know about Nygren, but this other guy is apparently better known in Sweden. Of course we've heard of him, but it's hard to tell if what you hear is fact or fiction. We've heard some pretty strange stuff."

"Probably fact," said Jansson.

"Quite the guy then. Sundell requested his file from Sweden, but it hasn't arrived yet. I'm sure you can help us with the same questions, but let's start from the beginning."

Jaatinen flipped on a slide projector. He pressed a wired remote and a picture of the crime scene appeared on the wall.

"The body was found in the storage yard of Rusanen's construction company. There was all kinds of junk piled on top of the body, but fortunately some workers picking up a disassembled crane wound up clearing it away. According to our initial investigation Rusanen was shot to death yesterday evening in the trailer located on the property. He was shot once in the head. Nobody heard the gunshot, so it's possible there was a silencer on the weapon. Rusanen was armed, but he never got the chance to use it."

"Apparently, Rusanen had arrived there voluntarily, since his car was on the property and it was locked. He was last seen alive at about noon that day in downtown Oulu while leaving his home."

Jaatinen pulled up a slide of the blood-stained trailer.

"Did he keep any money in the trailer?" asked Jansson.

"Apparently some, but only a few thousand euros. Still, we don't think we're dealing with a robbery.

We suspect the shooting is connected to drug trafficking. Ten pounds of amphetamines were found under the floor of the trailer, and we're fairly certain that Rusanen was the drug kingpin for all of northern Finland and even parts of Sweden. He was well connected to the Estonian and Russian mafias. Right now, we're working with Customs on a case where at least fifty pounds of Estonian amphetamines were brought into the country. The dope's been coming from Tallinn to Helsinki and paid for with stolen cars and snowmobiles. A month ago, one of Rusanen's couriers was arrested for possession of five pounds of amphetamines."

Sundell poured more coffee for Jansson and Huusko. Huusko used it to wash down another sandwich.

"Fantastic subs," he murmured.

"We've received intel that Rusanen's business was starting to get too big north of the Arctic Circle and he was planning to expand further south. The southerners weren't too fond of the idea, however."

Jaatinen's next slide was of the body itself. The victim lay on his stomach beneath a pile of cement-splattered concrete forms. A lone hand thrust out of the heap.

"Nygren doesn't take marching orders from the drug bosses. He wouldn't be thinning competition on their behalf," Jansson pointed out.

Jaatinen nodded.

"I agree that Nygren doesn't seem to fit the picture, but this other guy fits the profile for the killer. What do you think?"

"Maybe. But Raid doesn't carry out hits for fun. If he kills someone, he's getting paid. On the other hand, Raid has his own moral code. He doesn't approve of drugs. Maybe a disagreement just broke out over something and Nygren and Raid were forced to defend themselves."

"Whatever the motive might have been, one of them was there. We have an extremely reliable witness for the Mercedes, which was seen in the vicinity of the storage yard just before the estimated time of death. It's an almost perfect match. According to the witness, there were two people in the car, but we couldn't get any detailed descriptions."

Heikkilä jumped into the conversation for the first time.

"Rusanen is certainly unpleasant enough that he'd have plenty of enemies. If the car hadn't been seen, we'd have about a dozen other suspects."

"Unpleasant in what way?" asked Huusko.

"Extremely violent. According to our sources, some of his couriers have been forced to do jobs under threat of violence and many have been beaten pretty brutally. He's also threatened their family members."

"Then I guess the killer did us all a favor."

"You could say that, but only as a private citizen," Jaatinen conceded.

"Have there been any sightings of Nygren's Mercedes since then?" asked Jansson.

"Amazingly, no," said Jaatinen. "We figured the car would be easy to find, but that hasn't been the case. It's apparently been ditched somewhere."

"Who's the witness?"

"There's a junk yard on the neighboring property. One of the workers was cutting up a car in the yard and noticed the Mercedes. The guy happened to be a buff on old Benzes and recognized the model and even the sound of the engine: a three-and-a-half liter V8, just like Nygren's. The color matches too."

The next slide was taken at the morgue. Rusanen's body lay naked on the examination table. Both arms were tattooed from the wrists to the biceps. The bullet's entry point was clearly visible.

Jaatinen continued.

"According to Kempas' theory, Nygren and Raid are plotting some big job. Seems to me they're on some kind of tour of Finland, but as for why, we still don't know. In Turku, they stormed into some cult's church and threatened its leader with a gun. Then they beat up two ex-cons at a service station who were apparently demanding money from Nygren. Next they shot and wounded one of these men on Nygren's farm, and now Rusanen's murder. My fear is that things will really run amok if we don't catch them. Our goal is to gather every possible bit of information so we can anticipate their next move. They're not moving randomly; they seem to have a clear plan with a fixed route."

Jansson was starting to tire of the same old refrain.

"Kempas already knows my opinion, but apparently it doesn't jibe with his. Nygren's dying and wants to do some kind of farewell tour. Apparently, Sariola and Lehto found out about it and wanted an advance on their share of the inheritance. Raid and Nygren gave them as much of a whipping as they had to and then continued on their way. How Rusanen's murder fits into the picture, I have no idea. Maybe Rusanen owed Nygren some money and when he came to collect, Rusanen resisted."

Jaatinen seemed disappointed. He had been expecting something from Jansson that would advance the case.

"Kempas thinks it's possible Nygren made up the story about his illness so he'd have room to go about his business."

"Really? I understand we have confirmation from the hospital about the cancer, so unless Nygren's bribed the doctor and falsified the lab samples…"

"Still, Kempas apparently knows Nygren better than any of us. He mentioned he's been after the guy for more than twenty years."

"That's true," Jansson conceded.

A knock came at the door. A younger uniformed officer came into the room with a sheaf of paper in his hand.

"We got a fax from Stockholm."

Jaatinen took the papers and started leafing through them.

"It's the file on Nygren."

He dove back into the papers, found something interesting and began reading closely.

"According to this, Nygren and Raid met in Sweden. They were suspects in the robbery of a horse-betting track almost fifteen years ago."

"That's nice to know, but it's not much help," said Huusko.

"Nygren has an apartment in Stockholm and another in Spain. According to the Swedish authorities, he left for Finland a month ago… He was being treated for stomach cancer in the Karoliina Hospital."

"Can't these Swedes tell us anything we don't already know?"

Huusko picked out a third sandwich from the tray and poured himself another cup of coffee.

Jaatinen tossed the papers aside.

"Maybe it's best if we wait for Kempas and then have another meeting."

"Agreed," said Huusko.

He glanced at the empty sandwich tray.

"With another round of sandwiches, right?"

\* \* \*

Jansson and Huusko were checking into a hotel near the police station.

"You have a mini-bar?" was Huusko's first question.

"No."

"Dancing?"

"No."

"What about porn channels?"

The young female receptionist stared at Huusko coolly.

"There's a magazine stand just across the street. You can find some adult materials there."

Jansson and Huusko got adjoining rooms on the top floor.

"Huusko, stop into my room once you're unpacked. Let's have a little meeting before Kempas gets here."

"I just thought of something really important," said Huusko.

"What's that?"

"Are we getting overtime?"

Huusko got his things organized within ten minutes. Afterwards, he knocked on Jansson's door.

"Better than mine," Huusko said as he sized up the room. "What'd you wanna meet about?"

"The plan."

"What about it?"

"That maintenance man from the casino case. I got the name from Susisaari."

"And?"

"We're going to visit him."

"In Helsinki?"

"He lives near Rovaniemi now."

"You think he knows something about Nygren?"

"Kempas had marked all of Nygren's acquaintances on his map. One of the marks was near Rovaniemi."

Jansson looked at the name he'd written on the back of a business card.

"Keijo Hiltunen...runs an auto repair shop somewhere around there. Name ring a bell?"

"No."

"It should. He killed two people...two young women. The case was one of the most notorious of the sixties. The new age sociologists considered it a prime example of the connection between childhood social circumstances and criminal behavior. They made a correlation between unhappy childhoods and a tendency toward crime. He got out sometime toward the end of the seventies."

"How does that relate to Nygren?"

"I was coming back from a fishing trip in Lapland with Lieutenant Hedenius when we stopped to gas up. You know him, right? He investigated the Hiltunen case. Unlike me, he recognized the guy right away. I just couldn't connect a casino maintenance guy from Helsinki with a service station manager in Rovaniemi. Especially not twenty years later."

"Didn't they look into Hiltunen's background when they were investigating the shooting?"

"It didn't seem necessary. Now that I think of it, it was pretty odd that nobody recognized him back then, as notorious as he was. Maybe the name was too common, and it didn't pop up anywhere. Susisaari looked into his background when she found his address for me."

"How is it connected to this case?"

"When Hedenius told me about Hiltunen's story, he also told me that Hiltunen and Nygren had been cell mates. According to Hedenius, after being released, Nygren had gone to see Hiltunen and arranged for regular deposits to his prison account.

"That made Hedenius wonder, and he looked into it. He found out that Nygren and Hiltunen had gone to the same elementary school. Nygren was a few years older. It appears that Nygren also got Hiltunen that maintenance job."

"Why you think Nygren would go see this guy now?"

"Because Nygren's settling accounts, taking revenge and doling out rewards. He punishes Pastor Koistinen by exposing his sham in front of the church. Then he goes to see his estranged daughter and gives her a wad of cash. Next he's bent on vengeance again, and he targets Rusanen, who he knows from prison. What his motive was, I don't know. Nygren and Raid are headed north and Oulu was right on the way."

"Brilliant deduction, Holmes," said Huusko. "How come you didn't mention Hiltunen to Jaatinen?"

"Maybe a little competitive spirit."

"And I thought I knew you. You gonna tell Kempas?"

"I doubt it."

# 19.

The last time Jansson had stayed at the Hotel Pohjanhovi in Rovaniemi was several years earlier. At that time, he'd been returning from a fishing trip in Lapland with a couple of other detectives. Jansson wasn't a terribly avid fisherman, but never objected to having a rod and reel in his hand.

For him, the Lapland trip had been more of a chance to meet up with old friends. Jansson had met Captain Hedenius, who now worked at the Rovaniemi division of the National Bureau of Intelligence, while attending a management training program. Hedenius was a hard-core fisherman, but even he knew how to fish just for the fun of it.

At the start of their police careers, Hedenius and Jansson had walked a beat that spanned most of Helsinki's downtown area. Walking side by side in hefty police-issue oxfords for thousands of miles had bonded the two enough that Hedenius had served as best man in Jansson's wedding.

The Hotel Pohjanhovi had also played another important role in Jansson's life, and even made the list of his top romantic memories, a list that wasn't terribly long. In the 1960s, as a young officer, he had toured Lapland in his first car, a dark-green

Volkswagen beetle. The girl who had sat in the passenger seat would become his wife a few years later.

The summer had been cold and rainy, and since the heater in the car was broken, much of the trip was spent shivering. The tent had been even colder, as their sleeping bags never quite managed to dry in the damp weather.

The only consolation about the weather was that the gnats and mosquitoes were practically nonexistent.

The car's exhaust pipe had fallen off in the fells and they toured a beautiful mountainous region to the blistering drumroll of unmuffled exhaust. Only after fifty miles of incessant droning did they find help, and the pipe was patched up with pieces of sheet metal, hose clamps and asbestos tape.

By this time, Jansson had realized that the journey was slowly but surely approaching catastrophic failure. He tried to salvage what was left to salvage and called the Hotel Pohjanhovi from a roadside general store just off Highway 4, reserved a nice room and ordered a bottle of bubbly and some flowers.

The investment was taxing on Jansson's meager savings, but it doubled its value many times over. The relationship flowered, and six months later, they moved into their first apartment. A couple of years later they were married. Their first child was born...

Huusko tapped on the passenger side window.

"The Benz is in the hotel ramp and they signed in with Nygren's name like a couple tourists. If they're the kind of pros they're purported to be, then what the hell are they thinking?"

Huusko's agitation stemmed from the fact that, in his experience, wrong was right. He'd be fine if the Mercedes had stolen plates and Nygren and Raid had signed into the hotel as Pekka and Matti Virtanen.

"Let's find out."

"Just us two?"

"Just us two. I promised Raid we'd come alone."

"Well, there are promises…and then there are promises."

"I only make promises."

"I guess you're from the old guard. The rest are in the elephant graveyard."

"Nygren's not violent."

"Wishful thinking."

Nygren's room was the upstairs suite. Huusko cocked his weapon and kept it at the ready under his jacket.

"Let's go."

Jansson rang the bell, positioning himself in clear view in front of the peephole. The door opened and Raid appeared.

"Come in."

Jansson went inside, but Huusko hesitated momentarily. Raid eyed the hand beneath his coat.

"Peace and love," he said in English.

Huusko holstered his gun and stepped inside.

"Nice to see you," said Nygren.

He lay on a large double bed in a semi-seated position, fully clothed, with a huge pile of pillows behind his back.

"Pour yourselves something to drink… I can order something to eat, too, maybe some sandwiches…"

"No thanks," said Jansson. He poured himself some mineral water. Huusko opened a beer.

"Thanks for coming," said Nygren.

"I guess I'm curious."

Jansson slid the desk chair to a roomier spot and sat down. A syringe and a box of medication lay on the nightstand.

"You guys are on quite the tour."

Nygren chuckled.

"A farewell tour."

Huusko examined the syringe.

"Hard stuff."

"Prescription meds. You won't get me on drug charges."

"What, then?" Huusko replied.

"That's what we're here to discuss," Nygren said.

"There's nothing to discuss. You're suspected of murder and attempted murder. You think you'll get off by talking? And this other one too…"

"No. And that's not my intention."

Huusko looked confused.

"Huusko, we'd best listen first," said Jansson.

"Lieutenant Jansson is right, it always pays to listen," said Nygren.

Nygren took a sip from his water glass and scooted himself into a more upright position. His hair hung over his forehead and his face was pallid. The tumult of disease roiled behind his glossy eyes.

"Here's my offer… I'll confess to killing Rusanen and give you the evidence. You'll get the murder weapon and an exact description of what happened and why. Then the case is closed."

"But why?" Huusko asked.

"Rusanen was a violent psychopath—and smart— a dangerous combination. Not to mention he was a megalomaniac…trying to dominate the entire country's drug market and build his own mafia."

"Whose toes did he step on?" Huusko asked.

"You got it wrong. It wasn't a matter of snuffing out competition; it was a personal issue for me and a few friends. I was in the pen with him when he started building his organization. He called it his 'käng.' Guess his English wasn't that good. He forced people to join. The prisoners were made to smuggle in drugs unless they wanted their old ladies beaten badly enough to warrant a trip to the hospital. He couldn't boss me around so he ended up asking me to join the käng's leadership. I told him to eat shit. While I was on parole, he sent a torpedo after me, so I just sent my own back. Mine prevailed. It shocked the shit out of him…then he left me alone."

"Is that your torpedo over there?" said Huusko, nodding toward the window sill where Raid was sitting.

Raid sat motionless.

"No names."

"Go on," Jansson implored.

"I found out about the cancer six months ago while in Sweden. They started treatment there, but ongoing treatment could only promise me a few extra months. No thanks. I'd rather settle up with my friends and enemies and get my affairs situated."

"You have a cemetery plot yet?" Huusko asked.

"Huusko!" Jansson growled.

"Yes. A straight answer to a straight question."

"So Rusanen was one of these enemies?" Jansson speculated.

"Yes. He'd forced some friends of mine to work for him. They'd have rather gone straight, but Rusanen never gave them the chance. The only way was to bump him. A final favor, if you will."

"What about Sariola and the other incident in Turku?" Jansson asked.

"Those punks came after me because they knew I had money. They were right, but it's not for them. They came to my farm and I shot Sariola in the hand with a shotgun."

"*You* shot him? What'd you hire this torpedo for if you're always the trigger man?"

"I need a chauffeur."

"You're telling me this guy didn't even touch the gun?"

"That's right. You'll only find *my* fingerprints on the gun. He didn't even know where I was."

"Bullshit!"

Jansson glowered at Huusko.

A pained expression flickered across Nygren's face, but he gathered his composure.

"About Turku, I've known Koistinen for over twenty years. He's been a con-artist his whole life. I'm not one to judge, but Koistinen is about as appealing as dog shit a shoe. A few weeks ago, an old friend from Turku called asking for help, told me Koistinen had started up a church there and was milking the flock for everything they had. My friend's daughter had fallen for Koistinen's charms and went berserk once she realized he was rotating among five women. Koistinen had promised to marry her. The girl fell for it, sold her house and gave all her money to the church. Once she realized what Koistinen was up to, she was so upset she tried to kill herself and ended up being committed."

"What'd you do to Koistinen?" asked Jansson.

"He doesn't listen to reason and I wanted to take

care of it quickly. I just shook him up a little."

"A little? The guy shit his pants," said Huusko, "and what do you mean by just you? According to our sources there were two men, one older and well-dressed, and the other a scruffy-looking, wild-eyed assassin."

"What are your terms?" Jansson asked.

"Good. Let's get to the point. You get a full confession with complete evidence. We get a half-day's head start."

Huusko flew out of his chair.

"What!"

"Starting right now. We'll leave immediately and I'll be fair game by noon tomorrow."

"No way…"

"Huusko, take a deep breath and calm down. Let's think this over."

"If you arrest me now, you have nothing—no evidence, no weapon, no credible motive, not even probable cause, let alone something that would hold up in court. Maybe you'll find someone who saw a car like mine near the crime scene, but that won't do."

"What do you need a half-day's head start for?" Jansson asked. "Someone else on your hit list?"

"Personal matters. I won't be fleeing the country in this condition, nor do I want to. If I did, I wouldn't have waited here for you. I just want a few hours to move freely. There's an APB out on the Mercedes so we'd be stopped as soon as we left here."

"True," Jansson conceded.

"It's a trick," Huusko muttered.

Nygren's eyes flashed and he rolled up his sleeve to reveal tracks of inflamed injection points. He took the syringe off the nightstand, tightened a belt around his upper arm and thrust the needle into a vein.

"Does this look like a trick? Pretty soon I won't be able to hold my own shit any more than my piss. You think I'm gonna run off into the mountains in this condition? With young men, dogs and helicopters after me? I'm hardly a match for a trained parrot."

Huusko's expression softened.

"Sorry."

"Once I've taken care of my affairs, I'll call and tell you where you can find me."

"What about him?" Huusko nodded in Raid's direction.

"He hasn't done anything."

"What do you need him for, then?"

"As I said, it's getting hard for me to walk... I need a driver."

Jansson walked over to Raid. The men stared at one another.

"Is that it?" Jansson asked.

"That's it."

"You'll guarantee it."

"Yes."

"There's one problem...a big one. How do I explain to my colleagues that I took the liberty of freeing two wanted criminals?" Jansson asked.

"You don't need to," said Nygren. "Just tell them you've arrested me and you're checking out the crime scene with my help. Cancel the manhunt and we'll leave town at once. We'll be on our way and I'll call you by evening. Nobody needs to know we've been missing for a few hours."

"No, goddamnit," said Huusko.

"And you won't do anything criminal?"

Nygren put his hand on his heart. "I swear on my God-fearing mother's grave."

Jansson looked Nygren over. He could almost see death perched on Nygren's shoulder, patiently counting the hours, minutes and seconds. His sleeve was still up and Jansson could see the web of blue veins beneath his pale skin. It seemed as if even the tattoos on his arms would fade before the final fall.

"Deal."

Jansson glanced at Huusko, who nodded.

"But I'll piss on your God-fearing mother's grave if you split," said Huusko.

The doorbell rang. Raid went to the door and looked out the peephole.

"Looks like more cops."

Huusko went to take a peek and came back.

"Kempas and his boys. What do we do?"

"Lieutenant Kempas from Helsinki?" asked Nygren.

"That's the one."

"How did he find us here?"

"I don't know. Huusko, open the door."

Huusko opened the door and Kempas tromped in with his lackeys. He moved toward the far wall and stopped to look Nygren over.

"We meet again. It's been a while."

"How did you find us?" Jansson asked.

"Luckily I have some friends at the phone company. You got a call from this room."

"You traced the calls to my phone?"

"Not me, the phone company. You left Oulu so suddenly I figured you were on the trail."

"I don't need your help."

"There's no point in arguing. The main thing is

the criminals are in custody."

Kempas sat down on the edge of Nygren's bed.

"You really sick or you acting?"

"I really am. That make you happy?"

"One shouldn't mix work with personal feelings."

"True."

Kempas glanced at Jansson.

"What has he told you?"

"He confessed to shooting Rusanen and Sariola."

"Good, but why?"

"Because in my condition, even you could catch me," said Nygren.

"Why'd you shoot Rusanen…not that I have anything against it."

"It's a long story."

"We've got time."

Nygren sighed.

"Do we really need the whole police force here?" Jansson asked Kempas.

"I just wanna be part of the fun."

"We got here first. Go back to Helsinki; we'll bring Nygren later."

"The two of you would never manage if they tried something."

"They won't."

Kempas went back to badgering Nygren.

"You won't?"

"No."

"Do you really want me to leave?"

"I do, and thanks for offering."

"I'd have rather stayed to chat. It's been a long time."

Nygren and Kempas looked at one another. In a surprise gesture, Kempas held out his hand.

"No hard feelings."

Nygren took it and squeezed.

"Likewise."

Kempas turned to Leino and Lunden.

"Go wait in the car, I'll be down soon."

Kempas turned to Jansson. "Can I have a word?"

Jansson followed him into the hallway.

"I know that woman."

"Who?"

"Anna Wahlman, maiden name Heinäkoski…from the physical rehab center. As a friend and colleague, I'd advise you to stay clear of her. Same goes for Huusko."

Kempas studied Jansson's reaction.

"When she was travelling abroad once, her apartment was burglarized. Too bad, since the burglar took thirty thousand in jewelry and furs. Luckily, the insurance company covered it. Then there was a basement fire in the house. Too bad, since over twenty grand in valuables went up in smoke. Luckily, the insurance company covered it. Always resilient, Anna was hardly phased, and she started giving private care to a rich, elderly man. While the guy was in the hospital, his apartment was burglarized and some antique silver and paintings worth half a million vanished. Five years ago, Anna Wahlman divorced the man. For some reason, he was afraid of the repo man and had the house and cabin transferred into her name. And there they stayed. Apparently, the man wants his property back, but she doesn't want to give it up. So she's hiding out in the country, clinging to burly men for protection. A good-looking woman, I must admit, but if she gets a hold of your family jewels, it's all downhill from there. That's all."

Kempas waved his hand and departed.

Jansson and Huusko escorted the Mercedes about ten miles outside of town. Nygren sat in the back seat beneath a blanket.

"You know the risk I'm taking by letting you go," Jansson said.

"I do, and I appreciate it," Nygren replied.

"Drive safely."

"Let's move. Till tomorrow."

"Till tomorrow."

Huusko came up behind Jansson.

"Think this was wise?"

"Hopefully."

"Why'd Kempas give in so damn easy? It's not like him."

"I wondered the same thing," said Jansson.

"Maybe he's got some scheme. What did he wanna talk to you about?"

"Nothing important."

"Think we can get a few hours of sleep?"

"Maybe a whole night's worth."

# 20.

The autumn-blanched crowns of the birch forest seemed to surge like a golden sea. The road traversed a clear stream, which flowed from a glacial lake over five miles away.

The road climbed steeply, but the Mercedes mounted the hill effortlessly.

Further up, a barely visible side road, almost a trail, branched off the main. It led into the heart of a thin, low-lying birch forest.

Not wanting to drive into something he couldn't get out of, Raid closely examined the road. It sloped gently toward the stream and ended in a small clearing about a quarter mile from the main road.

The clearing was used for camping. Near the perimeter was a fire pit made of stones and a pile of rusty cans. Based on the labels, canned tuna and pea soup were top choices for campers.

Raid and Nygren got out of the car. Nygren took a look around.

"Beautiful."

He ascended a footpath leading through the trees. Raid walked behind him. The trail was overgrown in places, and Nygren had to bend the branches aside. After walking for about a hundred yards, he stopped for a rest.

"Tired yet?"

"You won't need to carry me, if that's what you're afraid of."

"Not afraid of that."

After about twenty yards, they came to a steep bank and Nygren slipped. Raid caught him before he could fall. Nygren exhaled hard and mopped the sweat off his forehead.

"Thanks."

He took a break for some time before continuing. They climbed for another fifteen minutes before Nygren found a spot that he liked. From there, they could see a sparkling lake in the valley and the summit of another fell opposite the lake. The stream they had crossed earlier rippled past only ten yards away, its wavelets splashing against the rocks.

"This will do."

He glanced about, looking for a place to sit, and chose a grassy tussock at the base of a small birch. Raid sat down next to him. Nygren gazed at him with a faint smile on his face.

"You were with me to the end after all..."

"Yep."

\* \* \*

Hiltunen climbed out of the grease pit and wiped his greasy hands on an equally greasy rag.

"Can't you guys leave people alone? Nygren did his time, just like me."

Hiltunen's voice sounded genuinely annoyed.

"We'll leave you alone as soon as you clear up a few things," said Huusko.

"What things?"

"Come on, you know."

"No, I don't."

"How much you wanna bet?"

Huusko held out his hand. Hiltunen stared at it and snorted.

Jansson put his hand on Huusko's shoulder.

"Huusko."

"It's not right to lie, especially to the cops."

"Let's just stick to the facts. We're investigating Nygren and we believe he's been here."

"Can I ask why?"

"He's been seen in the area," Jansson lied, though his conscience promptly scolded him.

Hiltunen took to examining a carburetor on the table. His fingers were thick and his nails chipped, but his touch was light.

"I got a right to know why you're after him, don't I?"

"We're investigating a shooting and a murder—two different cases."

"And Nygren was the triggerman?"

"We're not sure. We'd just like to interview him for starters. He's been placed at the crime scene, at any rate."

"Who got shot?"

"A guy by the name of Sariola."

"Oh...that asshole. Serves him right. And who got killed?"

"Rusanen, sound familiar?"

"You think Nygren killed Rusanen?"

"That's what we're trying to figure out."

Hiltunen shook his head.

"Nygren's no killer... I mean, he can hold his

own, but he'd rather use his head. Rusanen thought he could bully him around like the others, but Nygren was too tough, too smart. Rusanen had to leave him alone."

"Can you think of anything Nygren might have against Rusanen?" asked Jansson.

"That I don't know. I'd have thought it'd be the other way around...that Rusanen would've retaliated."

"Did they have any business in common?"

"Nygren hated Rusanen. Wouldn't touch him with a ten-foot pole."

"Why then," said Jansson.

"If Nygren shot those guys, he couldn't have picked two better targets. He always said doing time would almost be nice if there weren't shitheads like Rusanen and Sariola in every brig."

"We're not saying Nygren killed him. All we want is to hear his side of the story."

"You wouldn't be asking me if you didn't have some evidence."

"Maybe we do," said Huusko.

"I don't know about Sariola, but I heard Rusanen died and..."

Hiltunen's voice faltered momentarily.

"You heard? From who?"

"Must have been in the news."

"No, it hasn't."

Hiltunen's son peeked in the door.

"Dad, it's almost two, we should go."

Hiltunen glanced at the clock.

"Be there in a sec..."

The boy disappeared.

"I have a...an appointment... I have to go."

"We can drive you. We'll talk in the car."

Hiltunen went to a steel wash-up sink, slathered his hands with soap and started scrubbing them.

"Nygren was here yesterday, but he didn't stay but half an hour. Said he was going to Lapland to see the leaves."

"What did he want?"

"Nothing much…just stopped by as he was passing through."

"Was he the one who told you about Rusanen?"

"I don't remember."

"Was he alone?" asked Huusko.

"No, some other guy was driving."

"You know who he was?"

"No."

Hiltunen took his cap off, revealing the bald spot on the top of his head. He set the cap on the desk, stripped off his coveralls and hung them on a nail. The shine on his shoes was flawless, but even so, he spat in a paper towel and polished them.

"Is Nygren a friend of yours?"

"I have no friends… He's a nice guy, but I wouldn't call him a friend."

"Then how come he came to visit you in prison and sent money?"

"Don't ask me."

"And got you a maintenance job in Helsinki. You and I met when I was investigating that casino shooting."

Hiltunen took a closer look at Jansson's face.

"Yeah, I thought you looked familiar…"

"Did he get you that job?"

"I had just gotten outta prison. I figured nobody would know me in Helsinki and people would leave me alone. I needed a job and a place to sleep and Nygren set me up. He knew the owner of the casino."

"You two come from the same town, right?"

Hiltunen looked at Jansson, clearly surprised.

"We do?"

"What, you didn't know?"

"Hell no... If it's true, he must have moved away before we met...we didn't get to know each other until prison. He never told me where he was from..."

"Did he know where you were from?"

Hiltunen's son peered in the door worriedly.

"We're gonna be late."

"Just a sec. Wait in the car."

He disappeared again.

"I gotta go."

"First tell us the rest and we'll leave you alone," said Huusko.

Hiltunen gave in.

"Okay. Nygren told me Rusanen was dead. He'd heard it from somewhere."

"Is that what he came all the way out here to tell you? Did he mention the cancer?"

"What cancer?"

"That he has cancer and he's dying," said Huusko.

"Nygren has cancer?"

"You sure weren't very close friends if he hasn't told you."

The annoyance on Hiltunen's face turned to seriousness.

"This service station is up for sale... Nygren gave me a loan... He didn't mention about any cancer... I was just headed to the bank with my boy..."

"A guy shows up outta nowhere and gives you money. Doesn't sound quite right," said Huusko.

"I know… I thought the same thing, but the money was already in my account by morning. I'm fifty-seven years old, and spent sixteen of those years in prison for one mistake. This is my only and final opportunity and I'm damn thankful… Or would unemployment be a better alternative, or should I just string myself up…"

Hiltunen's voice cracked and he looked down at his hands.

"How much did he give you?"

"Fifty thousand."

"And he didn't even give you a contact number or an account number?"

Hiltunen stared at his hands in silence.

"Has anyone else come asking about Nygren? Fellow by the name of Kempas, for instance?"

"The cop?"

"Yes, the cop," Huusko replied.

"No."

"Did Nygren ever talk about Kempas?"

"Not this time."

"Did he tell you what Kempas has against him?"

"He has something against him?"

"That's how it looks. Any idea why Kempas hates Nygren so much?"

* * *

Nygren raked some fallen leaves together with his fingers and heaped them into a small pile. He stretched out on the ground with the leaf pile under his head. Though the sun was dazzlingly bright, he took off his sunglasses and handed them to Raid.

"Genuine Ray-Bans, they're yours."

Raid slipped them on.

"You never told me the story about these."

"It doesn't matter anymore. Now they'll have a new story that you can either tell or not tell."

Nygren took a wallet out of his coat pocket. He opened it, slipped a car key out of the coin pocket and pressed it into Raid's hand.

"The spare key to the Mercedes. It's yours now, you'll make your own story for it."

"Thank you."

Nygren dug around in his wallet some more and pulled out a folded receipt and a photograph.

"Your fee has been wired to your account. Here's your receipt."

Raid took the paper and shoved it in his pocket without looking at it.

Nygren clasped his hands over his chest so they cradled the photograph. Raid could see that it was the picture of Nygren's daughter with the black-and-white cat in her lap.

"When you were baptized, the pastor reminded us godparents of the responsibility we were taking on. He said a godparent's most important job is to keep his godchild on the path of righteousness. We godparents were supposed to live as good examples for our godchildren. I remember holding you in my lap and thinking, Poor thing…best not take any lessons from your old uncle. I saw your mom looking at me kind of stern, and I'm sure she knew what I was thinking. As you got bigger, things went just the opposite of the way they were supposed to. You started imitating everything I did, both good and bad, especially bad. I noticed it, but for some reason it gratified me and I couldn't be strict enough. I'll never forgive myself for that."

Raid took off the sunglasses. "I had so little to be proud of."

"I understand that now."

"When you came to visit, I wanted to take it all in. I'd tell anyone who'd listen that you were my godfather. I told them you were rich and lived abroad. The other boys were jealous because it seemed like you were from another planet. You drove an expensive car, had nice clothes and bought me the kinds of presents other kids never got."

"You only saw the glamorous parts, and I don't blame you. That's what I wanted to show you. And that's why I feel responsible for your turning out the way you did."

"I made that decision myself."

"I set an example and opened the door. You let a kid run loose in a candy store, you can't blame him for stealing."

"I'd have never made much of an upstanding citizen anyhow."

"You had a good father and an even better mother. Maybe things would've turned out different if they'd lived. You were too young to be on your own."

"Adversity was a good teacher."

"I know it's too late to be a good godfather, but I still have to try... I didn't want you along on this trip to be my driver or my bodyguard. Not much left of my body to protect and the Benz has always gotten me where I need to go. You're here because I want to show you the road I've taken, and that I regret every turn."

Nygren took Raid's hand.

"The truth is that I've been happiest when I've

lived an ordinary person's ordinary life. Gone to work in the morning, come home in the evening. Held my daughter in my lap, played with her and read her a bedtime story. Done everything considered dull then, not realizing it was the best life had to offer. Somehow I convinced myself I was destined for some other glamorous life full of riches and fame. And so I was never able to enjoy what I had."

"I've always been proud of you."

"But for no reason. I haven't done anything to make anyone proud."

"You rescued a church from a scam-artist and helped the kid with the big shoes. Those were good deeds."

"And I did them solely for selfish reasons...because I'm afraid. So I'd have something to put in the empty end of the scales. It's the same reason I'm preaching to you right now, even though it's fucking difficult for me. If I were you, I wouldn't listen to a single word. I would think, oh, the old man's rambling again."

"You don't owe me anything."

"I certainly do. And the more you follow in my footsteps, the more I owe you."

"Every man is responsible for his own life."

"Believe me...you're wrong. I am responsible for you, and you for someone else."

"I absolve you of all responsibility."

"I've always wondered why your mother asked me to be your godfather... She believed in me even when she knew what I was...the blackest sheep of the family."

"She was your sister. She knew you better than

anyone, better than you knew yourself."

Nygren fluffed up his leaf-pillow and found the most comfortable position possible, with his hands folded over his chest. He looked at Raid.

"The letter's in my pocket."

Raid nodded.

"And don't forget the follow-up inspection. That's part of the deal."

"Right."

"It's a good day to die," Nygren said in English.

Raid smiled.

"Didn't I say you'd do it?"

Nygren smiled and closed his eyes.

Raid slipped a pistol out of his pocket, held it just shy of Nygren's temple and fired. The echo rumbled over the fells.

Raid stood up, arranged the pistol carefully in Nygren's hand and fired it toward the sky. Then he picked up the empty casing and put it in his pocket. He took hold of the birch that was bowing over them and shook it, dropping a shroud of yellow leaves onto the body.

From somewhere off in the fells, Raid heard the approaching *thuk-ka-thuk-ka* of a distant helicopter. It closed in quickly, looked briefly for a landing spot, then touched down in a small clearing in the birches. The current from the rotors beat against the tiny trees.

The door of the helicopter opened and out hopped Lieutenant Kempas. The pilot shut off the engine and the roar began to die down. Kempas hurried over to Raid, pressing his hat onto his head. When he saw Nygren's body, he stopped and slowly took it off.

"I met your uncle in the hospital in Sweden a couple months back. He'd just found out he had but two months to live. I promised him a peaceful departure. Even though he didn't want me to, I've been trailing him. I wanted to be there if he got stopped before the end of the road. This looks like the end."

"That's right."

"Your uncle asked me to pray for him after he died. I made the mistake of promising, so I've been up many nights thinking about what I might say. I don't know how preachers think of a new sermon every single day."

"They get paid for it."

Kempas cleared his throat and folded his hands. He bowed his head and looked at the ground. Then he bent down next to Nygren's body and turned toward Raid.

"An autumn hike. Sure is beautiful weather."

Raid nodded.

"If I had my choice, I'd die on a day just like today…nothing wrong with the spot either. Not too many get a choice, though."

"Right."

"I'm guessing you don't need a ride," said Kempas.

He held out his hand. Raid hesitated before shaking it.

"Your uncle was a good man, better than most people knew. I knew him for twenty years."

Kempas climbed into the chopper and the engine roared to life. Then it rose into the sky and flew off over the fells.

\* \* \*

Hiltunen gaped at Jansson.

"Nygren doesn't hate Kempas. He thinks Kempas is a nice guy."

"Are we talking about the same Lieutenant Kempas?" Huusko demanded.

"Yeah, the undercover boss. Those two are friends."

"Fuck!"

"If ever cops and robbers were friends, those two are."

"You're full of shit!" Huusko roared.

Jansson shot Huusko a stern look.

"Huusko!"

"I'm tellin' you…they're friends. Nygren saved his life once."

"Kempas' life?" Jansson wondered. "When and where?"

"You should know, shouldn't you?"

"How's that?"

"If you investigated the casino shooting…"

"What happened there?"

"Don't you know?"

"No."

"Well, Kempas was trying to bust the casino along with Nygren and Salmi for illegal gambling. Those two owned the place. Kempas was still just a regular cop back then…not that he's ever been that regular. So he finds the place, stakes it out for a week, and arrests some professor. You couldn't get in without knowing somebody, so Kempas made the professor take him in… He gambles for a couple hours and then some guy walks in, recognizes Kempas, pulls a gun and is about to shoot. Nygren was there and stepped into the line of fire just as the guy popped one off. The bullet hit Nygren in the gut before Kempas managed to shoot the guy."

"So Kempas shot Luotola?"

"Don't know the guy's name, but he wound up in the hospital half-dead. Nygren said he and Kempas came up with a story for the cops. Nygren and the other guy kept mum and the cops bought it hook, line and sinker. Nygren and Kempas have been friends ever since."

"Have they met up since then?"

"Many times."

"When was the last?"

"Nygren said Kempas paid him a visit in Sweden not too long ago."

\* \* \*

"Think he's telling the truth?" said Huusko as they got back to the car.

"I knew Kempas was involved with it somehow and we investigated the incident together. Even back then I had the feeling he wasn't telling me everything, but it never occurred to me he might be conspiring with Nygren. I figured he was protecting one of his informants."

"Couldn't they identify the weapon based on the bullet? Kempas probably used a standard police-issue firearm."

"We determined the model and make, but plenty of people have the same weapon. Over a dozen police-issue guns had gone missing at the time, too. And we had no reason to believe Kempas had been at the casino."

\* \* \*

Huusko watched a low-flying helicopter approach in the rear-view mirror. The chopper swept overhead at an altitude of about thirty feet. Further up ahead, it circled and landed at a rest stop.

"I thought I saw Kempas," said Jansson.

"I had the same nightmare," said Huusko. He braked and coasted up the exit ramp toward the helicopter. Kempas stood next to it with his hat in his hand. He looked relaxed, like someone who'd spent his whole life flying around on the tax-payer's dime.

"It's Kempas alright."

Kempas smiled, looking somehow like a different man…softer.

"You must have been on an old trail if you went to see Hiltunen."

"Old, but hot," said Huusko.

"More like cold. Nygren's dead."

"Dead," said Jansson and Huusko at the same time.

"Shot himself in the mountains."

"What about Raid?"

"Gone."

Jansson was suspicious.

"That's it?"

"That's it. Nygren was on a trip to the fells to die the whole time. Some fancy of his. Raid was along to drive him there. Along the way, Nygren settled up with himself, paid virtue with virtue, and vice with vice."

"And what was your role?"

"I met him in Sweden while he was at the hospital. He told me he wanted to die in Finland and I promised to help. I suppose Hiltunen told you why."

"Yeah."

"Nygren saved my life…and he could've got me in deep shit. It's hard not to respect a man like that."

"What now?" said Jansson.

"He left a full confession and a gun. That closes Rusanen's case and Sariola's too. We have nothing on Raid."

"I guess not," said Jansson.

Kempas looked Jansson directly in the eyes.

"Now you know my secret. What are you gonna do?"

Jansson glanced at Huusko.

"Hardly seems anyone would be interested in such an old case."

"An old case," Huusko repeated.

Kempas nodded.

"Thanks."

With a wave of his hand, he signaled the pilot and the helicopter's rotors began to whirl.

"I can give you a ride to Helsinki," said Kempas.

"No, thanks."

He climbed into the chopper and gave a wave as he shut the door.

"I wish I could be there when he gives the chopper bill to his boss," said Huusko.

"Me too."

# 21.

Huusko dropped Jansson off at his house around six in the evening. Jansson took his suitcase out of the back seat and thanked Huusko for the ride.

"Best not to gripe about your back for a little while," said Huusko.

"Right."

Jansson saw the drapes flutter in the upstairs window. He climbed over the fence and cut across the lawn. On the way, he picked an apple, took a juicy bite and tossed the remains under the hawthorn hedge.

His car was parked in the driveway and the front door was unlocked. Jansson set his suitcase on the entry bench and kicked off his shoes.

"I'm home," he hollered from the kitchen.

On the kitchen table was a bottle of sparkling wine on ice, and next to the cooler was a small plate of crackers topped with smoked salmon and roe. Jansson inhaled one in a single bite and washed it down with wine.

He heard some music coming from upstairs and recognized Placido Domingo. The first checkmark was hanging on the stair railing: his wife's panties, black, little and lacy. There was no mistaking the invitation.

Jansson inhaled another cracker, took the plate in one hand, tucked the bottle under his arm, and took the wine glass in his other hand.

A black thigh-high stocking was dangling from the bedroom doorknob. The door was ajar enough that Jansson was able to bump it open with his knee.

His wife had drawn the curtains and left on only the bedside lamp. She lay on her right side in the classic come-hither position, dressed in something that should be banned for anyone under fifty.

The three tenors raised their tremolos to the highest imaginable frequency. His wife lifted her hand to her hip and caressed it.

"Show me what kind of shape they got you in now."

"You wanna cracker?" asked Jansson, offering the plate.

"No."

"What about some bubbly?"

"No."

"Isn't the music a little loud?"

"No. Aren't you a little overdressed?"

"Sometimes you think you know a person, but you really don't…"

"What are you talking about?"

"Lieutenant Kempas."

"Forget Kempas and pay attention to your wife."

Jansson set the bottle on the nightstand and the plate of crackers next to it. He loosened his belt and unsnapped his pants. He couldn't get any further before his wife yanked them down.

"What about foreplay?" Jansson asked.

"Forget it."
"Right down to business, huh?"
"Right down to business."

# 22.

The collection plate in Turku's Elia Church completed its rounds more brimming than ever. Complete forgiveness of sins, new hearts, washed in the blood of the lamb, new souls, as white as heavenly linen. New joy and jubilation as the sinners received grace. Verily, verily, was there good reason to slay the fatted calf and call the guests to partake in the joys.

Only the pastor was old. The same old suit, the same thick gold chain on his wrist, the same slick part in his hair, the same greed and cynicism.

Pastor Koistinen stood behind the lectern, his hands in the air, palms up.

"For my enemies have retreated, fallen to the ground and turned to dust in front of thine eyes. Thou hast granted me the authority and championed my cause. Sit on thy throne, oh righteous judge. My enemies have been destroyed, cast into eternal ruin, their cities overthrown, their memories vanquished…"

The double doors opened and Raid strode inside. He walked up the center aisle to the middle of the church. One by one, the voices hushed, and at last Koistinen came out of his rousing tirade.

Koistinen stretched out his arm and leveled a finger at Raid.

"I have received grace and a new life in heaven, you have no power over me…"

"You get a new wallet too?"

"Seek salvation, heal thyself and turn away from sin! Your life is as brief as the grass in the field; today it grows and tomorrow it's cut. God alone knows when the harvest will come."

"God and I."

Raid drew a gun from beneath his coat, cocked it and fired two quick shots into Koistinen's chest, directly into his heart.

Koistinen crumpled to his knees before pitching forward onto his face. Then he was no more. He was like the grass in the field, which yesterday grew and today was cut.

Raid turned and walked out.

In front of the building was an old Mercedes, a car with a tale. One day, he would tell the tale to someone who was entitled to hear it. And he would add his own parts to it and it would become richer.

He drove down the neon-tinged main street, through a sleepy suburb and banked to the right into the current of the highway.

## Also by Ice Cold Crime:

**Helsinki Homicide: Against the Wall**
**Jarkko Sipila**
**292 Pages, $11.95**

An abandoned house in Northern Helsinki, a dead body in the garage. Detective Lieutenant Kari Takamäki's homicide team gets a case that looks like a professional hit but they are perplexed by the crime scene.

Takamäki's trusted man Suhonen goes undercover as Suikkanen, a gangster full of action. In pursuit of the murderer, he must operate within the grey area of the law. But, will the end justify the means? Following in the footsteps of popular Scandinavian writers, Jarkko Sipila is introducing his critically acclaimed Takamäki series in the United States.

Jarkko Sipila is a Finnish author and journalist. He has been reporting Finnish crime news for MTV3 TV News and the Helsingin Sanomat newspaper for almost 20 years. He has written 11 novels and co-wrote a TV- series "Detectives Don't Sing" based on the Takamäki-books. The pilot episode drew almost a million Finnish viewers.

*Helsinki Homicide: Against The Wall*, the winner of the 2009 Finnish Crime Novel of the Year Award, is the first of Jarkko Sipila's nine Takamäki-novels to be translated into English.

## Also by Ice Cold Crime (continued):

**Helsinki Homicide: Vengeance**
**Jarkko Sipila**
**335 Pages, $12.95**

Tapani Larsson, a Finnish crime boss, walks out of prison with one thought on his mind: Vengeance. Wanting to reclaim his gang's honor and avenge those who have wronged him, Larsson targets Suhonen, the undercover detective who put him in prison. Meanwhile, Suhonen's best friend, an ex-con himself, wants to wash his hands of crime, but in the process, is driven deeper into it.

With the help of his boss, Lieutenant Takamäki, and the National Bureau of Investigation, Suhonen hunts for the loose thread that could unravel the entire gang. But with every string he pulls, he flirts with death itself.

*Helsinki Homicide: Vengeance* is another thrilling read from Sipila. It is the second of his books to be translated into English. The first, *Helsinki Homicide: Against the Wall*, won the 2009 Finnish Crime Novel of the Year Award.

Jarkko Sipila is a Finnish author and journalist. He has been reporting on Finnish crime for 20 years, has written 11 books, and co-wrote a TV series based on the Takamäki books. Through realistic characters and story lines, he explores current topics surrounding life in contemporary Finland.